THE EARL'S UNSPOKEN LOVE

A REGENCY ROMANCE

ROSE PEARSON

LANDON HILL MEDIA

THE EARL'S UNSPOKEN
LOVE

PROLOGUE

*T*here she is.

Marcus was unable to express how joyfully his heart sang at the sight of Lady Almeria. It seemed to still in his chest, his breath coming raggedly as he saw her smile. He and Lady Almeria had been friends all through childhood, but it had been some time since he had last laid eyes upon her. Now, it was as though the candles in the ballroom glowed a little more brightly, as if the music from the orchestra played a little more sweetly, simply because he was looking at her. Her dark hair curled over her shoulder in one large ringlet, the rest pulled away from her oval face. Her rosebud lips were curved into a smile, her hand going to her mouth as she laughed at something her friend had said – and Marcus' lips lifted as though he were a part of the conversation, as though he too were enjoying the merriment.

I have been apart from her for too long.

A troubling thought passed over his mind and he pulled his eyes away from her.

What if she is already betrothed?

News had not reached him of her betrothal but that did not mean that it had not taken place. He had been unable to attend London the previous Season due to complications with his estate - some of the fields were flooded with an unexpected rainfall and he had been forced to set aside frivolity for the sake of his tenants and his finances. Aware that it had been Lady Almeria's coming out, he had been deeply frustrated to have to remain at his estate, but there had been no other choice. However, he had prayed very often that he would not be too late, that she would not find herself a husband – and as yet, his prayers seemed to have been answered.

Might he yet find himself much too late? It had been a fortnight since the Season had begun, and much could happen in that time – especially with someone as beautiful, as refined, and as kind-hearted as Lady Almeria! Taking a breath, Marcus set his shoulders, and lifted his chin, pushing away his fears. He had heard nothing as yet about any betrothal, had heard no whisper that she was even being courted by anyone, thus far. He had to hope, had to pray for a chance that she might look at him in a different way – in the way that he had always looked at her.

With a nod to himself, Marcus pushed away his nervousness as best he could. He had no need to hold himself back. Lady Almeria was his friend. They had known each other for many years now, and it would be foolish to stay away from her out of the fear that he might hear the very worst of news. If she discovered that he was present and had not come to greet her, she might wonder at it, questioning why he had done so, and finding herself displeased with him. That was the last thing he desired.

With a slight lift of his chin and with confidence in his step, Marcus made his way directly across the ballroom.

Lady Almeria's gaze flicked to his face and then away again, only to return in an instant. Her hazel eyes flared wide, and she put one hand to her mouth, catching her breath.

"Marcus!"

He smiled broadly at her whisper and bowed low.

"Almeria - I mean *Lady* Almeria."

A flush of embarrassment touched his cheeks, only for the lady to laugh.

"I think I shall easily be able to forgive you, for we are great friends, are we not? We have been friends for almost as many years as we have been alive! Therefore, I think it perfectly suitable for you to call me Almeria."

She put her hand out to him, and Marcus grasped it quickly, the warmth in his face now coming from a different feeling entirely.

"Indeed, we are, Almeria." He smiled at her and looked into her eyes, aware of his heart picking up its pace. "You cannot know how glad I am to be in your company again."

Her eyes lit up.

"And I yours," she promised softly. "Although I had hoped to see you last Season. You were not present in London, and I missed you excessively."

"No, I was not." Catching the curious glances of her companions, he shrugged his shoulders, keeping his explanation for another time. "But I am here now and have every intention to stay in London for the entirety of the Season."

"As do I." Almeria smiled softly. "Now, would you ask me to dance? It has been some time since we have done so, but I am certain that we will remember how!"

A sudden tightness grasped his heart, squeezing it as he accepted the dance card from her. How little she knew of how her nearness affected him, how much her closeness to him as they danced would send his heart into a flurry! His very soul seemed to dance about him with delight as he wrote his name down for her cotillion, and thereafter the waltz, relieved that it had not been taken. With a small smile, he handed the card back to her.

"I hope you do not mind that I have taken your waltz. After all, it has been some time since we have danced together, as you said."

Lady Almeria looked down at her dance card and then smiled.

"No, indeed. In fact, I am a little relieved that you have taken the waltz, for there are so many gentlemen who, when dancing the waltz with me, are inclined to tread on my toes or grasp my hand far too tightly. Indeed, there are even some who think it a suitable moment to whisper certain things into my ear, none of which I am grateful for. I am sure that you understand." Marcus said nothing but nodded, thinking silently to himself how much he should like to whisper certain things into Almeria's ear. "I shall be very glad to dance with a friend." Reaching out, she touched his hand with hers for just a moment. "I am so *very* glad to see you." Marcus managed a smile, although his heart began to slow its quick pace. "Indeed, I think it is a very good thing that I shall have a gentleman friend here this Season," she continued, as the happiness which had bloomed in Marcus' heart slowly began to wilt. "You shall be able to tell me all about the various gentlemen of the *ton*, and if any of them appear to be at all interested in my company, I shall ask you of them."

Marcus managed a tight smile, a faint relief pushing away some of his sorrow.

She is not betrothed as yet, then.

"Of course..."

She smiled in response to his words, and then one of her

friends – who had not yet been introduced to Marcus – murmured something to Lady Almeria, who smiled and shrugged.

"And of course, I must now introduce you to my friends. They are all wondering who you are and why I have not spoken of you as yet!"

She quickly began to do so, but Marcus barely registered a single word. All the hopes which had begun to build within him now cracked and shattered. Lady Almeria did not see him in the same way that he had seen her for so long.

Time had changed nothing.

She did not expect, perhaps did not even want, anything more than friendship - and that sent a knife into Marcus' heart.

CHAPTER ONE

"*I* see Lord Coppinger is to dance with you again."

Almeria immediately laughed.

"Yes, but that is only Marcus."

Seeing Lady Yardley's eyebrows lift, Almeria quickly explained.

"You will think it odd for me to refer to him so informally, I am sure, but he and I have been friends since childhood. We practically grew up alongside one another and indeed, I think of him almost as one of my brothers. His father and mine were friends, and since his estate bordered my father's, we spent many hours together – very often outdoors until my mother insisted that I spend a little more time pursuing all of the things which were required of young ladies!" Her heart warmed with the happy memories which flooded her. "Even then, Marcus was always ready to spend time in my company. He and I were even given the same dancing master so that we might learn together, although I think we infuriated that poor gentleman a great deal with our nonsense!"

"I see." Lady Yardley smiled warmly. "How wonderful

it must be to have someone whose friendship you have enjoyed for so long. I assume that you know each other very well."

Almeria nodded.

"Yes, very well, although I have not seen him for a few years, since I have been in London for the Season with my elder siblings, and he has had a great deal of responsibility on his shoulders with taking on the title after his father died."

"Then you would say that he is a responsible gentleman?"

"Oh yes. He is an excellent gentleman in every way, I think." Her heart softened all the more. "The very best of fellows, I would say." Lady Yardley gave her a long look, and Almeria flushed and looked away, somewhat uncomfortable. "There is nothing of that sort between us, I assure you," she found herself saying, as though she needed to somehow defend herself when it came to Lord Coppinger.

Lady Yardley smiled.

"Of course. I did not mean to tease you. It is good to have a gentleman as close as a brother, for you will value his friendship a great deal, I am sure. Though might I suggest that you do not refer to him as 'Marcus', but rather by his title when you are in company." Lady Yardley pressed her hand. "I say such a thing not to embarrass you, but only because I do not want anyone to think you are overly familiar with him for any other reason other than friendship." Tilting her head, her eyes brightened. "But if he is as amiable as you describe him to be, perhaps you ought to consider him for one of your friends – provided he is a gentleman willing to consider falling in love!"

Almeria opened her mouth to say that Lord Coppinger would be an excellent match for any one of her friends, but the moment that she opened her mouth, the words were taken from her lips and blown away. It was as if someone had stolen her breath, leaving her with an uncomfortable prickling sensation running through her frame and a heavy weight dropping low into her stomach. Lady Yardley frowned, clearly waiting for an answer, and perhaps confused as to why none came.

Forcing the words out, Almeria demanded silently to herself that she smile.

"Yes, of course."

It was all she could say, but it was enough, for Lady Yardley smiled back, her frown gone.

"I am very pleased to hear it, Almeria. He looks to be a very pleasant fellow."

Almeria only half listened to Lady Yardley's remarks, wondering at her strange reaction to Lady Yardley's question. There had been no reason for her to react in such a fashion, for it was more than reasonable for Lady Yardley to question whether or not Lord Coppinger would be a suitable match for one of Almeria's friends. After all, excellent gentlemen were a little hard to find upon occasion, and she knew for certain that Marcus was a truly excellent fellow. Why should she mind if any one of her friends became better acquainted with him than she? Surely she should be glad that they had found happiness together.

But all the same, there was something deeply unsettling about the idea of Lord Coppinger being wed to one of her friends. She could not quite understand it, and the more she thought of it, the less she understood. It must be, she considered, only because they were such great friends that she found herself so concerned.

"Indeed, I should think it would be a very pleasant thing if your friend was wed to another dear friend."

Lady Yardley's words floated in towards her heart, but they did not bring Almeria any comfort. Rather, she found herself scowling, as though the thought of having one of her friends wed to Lord Coppinger was most displeasing. After fighting to arrange her features into a much more pleasant expression, she finally managed to do so, just as the very gentleman in question came toward her. Her heart lifted suddenly, but she turned her gaze away sharply, a little embarrassed by her reaction.

"Lady Yardley, this is my dear friend, Lord Coppinger."

"So it is." Lady Yardley smiled, and Almeria quickly made the introductions, seeing how Lady Yardley's keen eyes took in Lord Coppinger's features. Did she find him pleasing? To Almeria's eyes, Marcus was not at all unhandsome. Rather, with his somewhat stocky frame, his bright smile, and cloudy grey eyes, to her he was a very handsome gentleman indeed - although she had never allowed herself to consider his features with any great depth of feeling. "And you were absent from last Season, I understand."

Hearing Lady Yardley's question, Almeria concentrated her attention on Lord Coppinger. He had said to her that yes, he had been absent, but had not given any reason for it. A dark thought pushed itself into her mind. Was he perhaps already married? Was it that he had been on his wedding trip the previous Season and had now come to inform her that he was in fact, wed? Perhaps his wife was soon to be in her confinement, and thus he had come to London with her for a short time of enjoyment before such a thing began. Could it be that she was here with him, and as yet he had not had the opportunity to tell Almeria?

Her eyes closed tightly.

Please do not let it be so.

"Yes, I was absent last Season, although I very much wished to be here."

Almeria wrestled against a tightness in her throat. Her heart was beating rather painfully, her hands clasping together, her fingernails digging into her palms. Surely it could not be that Lord Coppinger was already wed?

And if he is, why am I so upset by even the thought?

"There had been unexpected flooding in some of my fields," he continued, looking directly at Lady Yardley. "My tenants are most important to me, and given that my livelihood is dependent upon how successful my estate is, I spent the spring and summer doing all that I could to make certain that we could salvage as much as possible." He shrugged. "I did not manage to save all of my crops, but we did save enough for a satisfactory harvest."

So loud was the breath of relief that came from Almeria, both Lord Coppinger and Lady Yardley looked at her at once – Lady Yardley with a little more concern than Lord Coppinger, certainly, but Almeria quickly then had to turn the sound into a cough. Her face flooded with heat as she flapped one hand in Lord Coppinger's direction, pretending that all was well.

"Forgive me, I lost my breath for a moment." It was the most foolish of explanations, but it was the one she gave, nonetheless. For a little longer, they both studied her, with Lord Coppinger speaking words of concern, but Almeria quickly smiled just as the announcement for the waltz spread out across the ballroom. "The waltz." Keeping her smile fixed, she accepted Lord Coppinger's arm and then smiled at Lady Yardley. "Pray excuse me, Lady Yardley."

"But of course." Lady Yardley smiled and waved one hand as though pushing them away. "It was very nice to meet you, Lord Coppinger."

"As I was glad to meet you," he murmured, before taking Almeria away.

Still embarrassed by her reaction to Lord Coppinger's explanation about the previous Season, Almeria remained silent as he led her to the center of the room. Quite why she had responded so was completely inexplicable, and yet that sensation lingered still. She was so utterly relieved to hear that he had not been absent because of a bride or a family of his own. She had responded in much the same way when Lady Yardley had suggested that one of her friends might be introduced to Lord Coppinger, finding herself recoiling inwardly, and then overcome with relief when the matter had been dropped and pushed away. The strange sensation turned into an inexplicable one, for it was not something she had ever needed to consider before.

"You are a little quiet, Almeria. I do hope that you are quite well." Lord Coppinger turned to face her, releasing her from his arm. "If you are unwell or fatigued, we do not have to dance the waltz."

"Certainly we do!" Almeria's heart stung at the thought of being set aside from him. "No, I shall hear none of it, Marcus. I am perfectly well, I assure you."

His gaze caught hers for a moment, still obviously concerned for her – and her breath caught in her chest, seeing the swirling in his grey eyes. The next second, however, he smiled and nodded, and the moment passed, assuring her that she was not about to be left abandoned at the side of the ballroom while he stepped out with another.

When did I become so eager to be in his arms?

"I do not remember the last time we stepped out together." The music began and he bowed as Almeria curtsied before he stepped forward to take her into his arms. "Do you recall we often had to learn, together, how to dance the steps? My dance master was deeply frustrated with us both!"

Remembering it all with perfect clarity, Almeria could not help but laugh as they began to step across the floor in perfect unison with one another.

"That is because we did not take his instruction seriously at all," she reminded him as he grinned down at her. "I think he found us most displeasing, for we did nothing but laugh and fall about, rather than heed anything he told us."

"But he taught as well enough, for see how splendidly we waltz now!"

Almeria's heart was overflowing with a happiness she had not experienced in some time. The way that they stepped out together reminded her of the past, of the many joyous hours she had spent in his company. Lord Coppinger was a fine gentleman, and she was glad to be able to call him a friend.

"I have missed you."

Quite where those words came from Almeria did not know, for she had not anticipated speaking them aloud. But yet they lingered, and she watched his eyes, saw his gaze soften as his arm tightened just a little more around her waist.

"I have missed you also, Almeria. More than I can express."

No further conversation passed between them and, as the dance came to its conclusion, Almeria found herself smiling up at her friend. She did not want the moment to end so quickly and hoped it would linger, but before she knew it, his hand was gone from hers. He released her gently from his embrace, and they stood apart from each other once more. Lord Coppinger inclined his head, as did she – and then he offered his arm, and their time together was at its end. Taking his arm, Almeria asked him to take her back towards Lady Yardley, fully aware that her mother and father were standing somewhere nearby, but they were quite contented for Lady Yardley to be her companion for the present. It allowed her mother to gossip with her many friends, and her father no doubt had already taken himself to the card games which were happening in another part of the house.

"Do you intend to stay in London for the rest of the Season?"

Lord Coppinger nodded, glancing at her as they ambled slowly forward.

"Certainly, I have every intention of remaining here. After all, a gentleman must find himself a wife, must he not?"

Stumbling, Almeria flushed as Lord Coppinger caught her.

"Forgive me, I..." His words had hit her hard, and she shook her head. "I am quite all right." A quick look in his direction caught his concerned gaze. "You truly seek a bride?"

Lord Coppinger nodded to her.

"Of course I do, Almeria. I must. It is the requirement of every gentleman if he is to perpetuate his family line and pass on his title. Thus, I must have an heir."

Something tied itself into a knot in her throat, and she swallowed it away, forcing it down as she attempted to smile.

"Yes, of course, you are right. You have always taken responsibility seriously."

"It seems we shall both be doing the same thing this Season, then." A wry laugh came from Lord Coppinger, but

Almeria could not join in. "You are here looking for a husband, and I am here looking for a bride. Let us hope that we shall both be successful."

Almeria tried to repeat the sentiment, but the words stuck to the roof of her mouth and refused to be released.

Thankfully, she was saved from having to say anything further by Lady Yardley's quick conversation. As she stood, still arm in arm with Lord Coppinger, Almeria found herself in a state of great disarray. Something very strange was occurring within her. Ever since Marcus had set foot into the ballroom, her certainty, her sureness, and even her poise had begun to crumble.

Now, to hear that he was within London to find himself a bride sent her into an ever greater turmoil... but exactly what she wanted to do about it, Almeria did not know.

CHAPTER TWO

"*I* assume you saw Lady Almeria last evening?"

Marcus rolled his eyes.

"Yes, I saw her. I believe you also saw me dancing with her, so I do not know why you are asking."

His friend chuckled.

"Yes, I saw you both. Might I ask if you still have a great affection for her? And, given that you confessed as much to me last Season, when you were absent from London, when do you intend to confess it to her?"

Marcus shook his head.

"You know very well, Trevelyan, that I have no intention of telling her any such thing at present. I have only just become reacquainted with her!"

"And why should that prevent you?"

Marcus threw up his hands, narrowly avoiding an older couple walking arm in arm as they strolled past them in St James's Park.

"Because she very clearly considers me only as a friend, at present, just as I have always been. I am nothing of any particular interest to her, and indeed she did not express any great hope of seeing me again. There was mention of taking walks here and there, or of stepping out together, not in any capacity. Therefore, I must consider what I am to do."

Lord Trevelyan turned his head, pausing for a moment and putting one hand out so that Marcus was forced to stop

"Did you, might I ask, ask her any of those things? Did you tell her you would very much like to take tea with her, or did you suggest that you walk together in the park, as you so clearly were waiting for her to do?" Marcus blinked. He tried to give an answer which would satisfy Lord Trevelyan, only to realize that he had come up with no answer whatsoever. His friend chuckled wryly and shook his head. "You cannot expect her to do so if you are unwilling to do the same. Besides it is not usual for a lady to express such hopes."

"Yes, but she is not just any young lady," Marcus responded quickly, continuing their walk. "She is Almeria, she is my friend, and we have often spoken to each other in such terms. If she wanted to meet with me, then she would express it."

"But you are not children any longer." Lord Trevelyan sighed and shook his head. "You say that it has been some years since you have last seen her, and no doubt, in that time, you also have changed in many ways. Is it not reasonable to think that she has changed also?"

Considering this, Marcus let the answer fall as nothing more than a sigh from his lips. Yes, he considered, it was quite reasonable to think that Lady Almeria might have changed a little, but he did not like to consider it. To his mind and his eyes, from what he had seen thus far of her, she appeared to be very much the same beautiful, engaging, delightful young lady she had always been to him.

"Even so, I think she would still have the same openness with me as we have always shared... but I will not confess my heart to her as yet."

"And now I think I shall have to convince you to do so." Sighing heavily, his friend passed one hand over his eyes. "I was hoping that I would not have to, but given you seem to be entirely disinclined towards pursuing the young lady, if I do not persuade you to act, then you will find yourself heartbroken. And then I will be forced to comfort you in as many ways as I possibly can. No doubt you will remain heartbroken for some time, returning to London Season after Season, declaring that there is none as proper, none as delightful, none as beautiful as Lady Almeria. Meanwhile, she will be quite happily settled with another gentleman, with a family of her own, and your heartbreak will not even be known to her."

This painted a picture that was both bleak and also a little mirthful at the same time, and Marcus ended up chuckling.

"You paint a very dark picture indeed, my friend."

"I say this only so that I will not have to carry the weight of your heavy-heartedness around with me for the next few years." Lord Trevelyan grinned, then shook his head. "You will simply have to do a little better, old boy. I would encourage you not to give up on the young lady. Do not give up on your feelings either, for they are of the greatest importance. It is not very often that a gentleman finds himself entirely besotted with a young lady, I can assure you, especially not for so many years."

Marcus cleared his throat, an uncomfortable prickling running over his skin.

"Sometimes I regret being as open with you as I have been."

"But I am glad of it. We are as close as two brothers might be. Indeed, I think even my own sibling does not share with me the things you do."

Smiling, Marcus looked straight ahead.

"And you do offer excellent advice, I will admit to that." Marcus took a breath and let it out slowly, considering. "I do not know what I should do. You are right, my heart *is* filled with Lady Almeria. But if she thinks of me only as her friend and companion, as I have always been, then what else is there for me to do but accept that?"

"Ah, but you cannot know for certain." Lord Trevelyan chuckled at Marcus' sharp look. "Who can know a lady's heart but the lady herself? She may be hiding as much from you as you are from her! And what then? What if, in looking back, you wish you had given a little more time to the lady? What if you had given enough time for her to consider how she felt, rather than simply accepting the assumption that she could not ever see you in the same light as you see her? Would you not turn into yourself, forever filled with regret, wondering about what might have taken place if you had only waited?"

Loath as Marcus was to admit it, all Lord Trevelyan said was worth considering - though what that meant in practical terms, he could not quite say.

He let out a low hiss of breath.

"I see your point. Do you have any suggestions as to what I ought to do?"

"Must I tell you everything?" Lord Trevelyan laughed, slapping Marcus on the shoulder. "Very well - what you must do is find a way to ensure that the lady knows of your affections while at the same time, waiting for the right moment to inform her of them."

Marcus threw out his hands, rolling his eyes in exasperation.

"That is no help whatsoever! I have very little idea of what I am to do."

Lord Trevelyan chuckled.

"I was not finished yet. My suggestion would be to send her flowers."

Marcus paused for a moment in their walk.

"Flowers?"

Surely every gentleman sent flowers to young ladies! What difference would such a thing make?

"Yes," Lord Trevelyan grinned. "All young ladies love flowers. They are seen as a sign of interest, and I believe that various flowers have different meanings. You might begin by sending some that speak of your admiration only to then proceed with ones which speak of your love for her."

He lifted an eyebrow as if waiting for Marcus to deny that he had such a depth of feeling but Marcus did not even protest.

"Flowers," he muttered again as Lord Trevelyan nodded. "It is an idea." Considering this quietly, Marcus began to nod, one hand rubbing at his chin. "Yes, I can see how such things might work. Then, in due course, I –"

"You tell her of your feelings," Lord Trevelyan confirmed. "When the time is right, and when you feel ready, of course. Things might have altered between you by then, already."

Again, Marcus considered this, finding the idea to be a pleasing one.

"Yes, I can see that flowers might work after all!" Grinning, he slapped his friend on the shoulder before they continued their walk. "Yet again you have proven that your advice is well founded. My dear friend, I am profoundly grateful for it."

"I am glad to hear it." Lord Trevelyan glanced across at him, still smiling. "The only question which remains is what flowers you are to send to the lady first."

"My friend states that some flowers speak of various emotions."

A little tongue-tied, it took Marcus a few moments to find the correct words, though the young woman behind the counter did not seem to mind, for there was a slight flush to her cheeks, as though she were very pleased indeed to hear him speak so.

"Yes, that is true." Turning, she picked up a tulip, a lily, and a rose. "For example, a tulip speaks of friendship – purple ones of admiration; a lily of sympathy – for an innocence has been restored to the soul of the one departed – and the rose, of love."

Marcus nodded, passing his gaze over the flowers. He was not about to send lilies, of course, but tulips certainly would suffice. Perhaps he might send her a bouquet every day or so, beginning with tulips and then slowly replacing them with roses, until there was nothing but roses for her to keep.

"And do you think the young ladies of society understand such things?"

A light flicker of heat rose in his face as he looked again at the young lady behind the counter, only for her to laugh softly.

"I don't think you would find a young lady who would

not know these things, my Lord." Her smile was soft. "You needn't worry."

His decision made, Marcus gestured to the tulips.

"Might you send a bouquet of these fine looking purple tulips?"

"Certainly, my Lord." She smiled. "We have many colors. Do you have any other particular color in mind? Or do you wish only the purple ones, with nothing to add to the effect?"

Marcus waved his hand.

"I fear I would choose poorly. I shall leave such things to you." Again, the lady smiled and nodded, reaching for her paper and a pencil. "And who am I to send these to?"

Quickly, Marcus was about to give Lady Almeria's name and state that she was the daughter of the Marquess of Fairburn, only to recall something important.

"Before I do, might I ask for your discretion in this?"

The young woman lifted her eyes to his.

"What do you mean?"

"I do not want my name to be attached to these flowers. Even if she should come to ask you, I would require your silence on the matter." The young woman's eyes flared, her lips pinching, but she nodded, saying nothing by way of response. "That does not mean that I am sending these flowers to anyone I ought not to be." Suddenly afraid the young woman thought him a rogue, sending flowers to a lady already wed, Marcus tried to explain, pushing one hand through his dark hair. "I wish my considerations to remain private at present until I am ready to declare myself. I want her to know how highly I think of her, that I admire her excessively, so that when the time comes to express my heart, she will know just how long I have held her in great affection."

Slowly, the pinched look faded from the young woman's expression and a tiny smile returned.

"I quite understand." From the warmth in her tone, Marcus trusted that she believed him. "I will keep your name from these flowers and keep my silence should she ask me anything."

Her pencil hovered over the paper, one eyebrow lifting.

Marcus smiled, satisfied all was well.

"Then please send them to Lady Almeria, daughter to the Marquess of Fairburn."

The young lady nodded, perhaps recognizing the name.

"A very admirable young lady."

Nodding, Marcus let his mind fill with thoughts of her.

"Yes, a very admirable young lady indeed."

CHAPTER THREE

"*L*ady Almeria."

The butler gestured for the footman to enter, and he walked in at once, bringing with him a beautiful bouquet of flowers. Immediately, her mother let out an exclamation, while Miss Madeley, her friend who had joined Almeria for the afternoon, simply clapped her hands.

"This is the fifth bouquet you have received this week!" Lady Fairburn exclaimed. "How wonderful!"

Secretly pleased, Almeria reached out both hands to take the bouquet from the footman, lifting it to her nose and inhaling the fragrance.

"Tulips. How lovely." Smiling, she handed them back to the footman, knowing that he would then go to arrange them somewhere suitable. "And the card?"

The butler shook his head.

"There was no card, my Lady."

"No card?" she repeated, blinking in surprise. "Why, this is the second time that I have received flowers without a note to say who they are from. Do you think..." She cast a glance towards her mother and then to Miss Madeley. "Do you think that the card has been lost?"

Her mother began to speak, clearly irritated with whoever had delivered the flowers, chastising them for dropping the note, even though they were not present in the room to hear her. Miss Madeley, however, tilted her head.

"You say that you have received *two* bouquets of tulips?" Speaking slowly, clearly, considering as she spoke, she narrowed her eyes a little as Almeria nodded. "And neither of these bouquets have had notes with them?"

Almeria opened her mouth to say no, only for her eyes to flare as she realized what her friend was suggesting.

"You mean to say that you believe whoever sent these flowers deliberately kept his name from them?"

Lady Fairburn waved a hand, snorting lightly.

"Preposterous! What would be the reason for that?"

Miss Madeley did not flare with any indignation, but only smiled.

"To make him all the more mysterious," she answered, as Lady Fairburn's expression of ridicule slowly faded. "He is keeping all knowledge of himself away, so that Almeria will begin to think of him a great deal... even without knowing who he is."

Much to Almeria's surprise, her mother immediately agreed, changing her view so rapidly that Almeria had to take a few moments to gather herself.

"Yes... yes!" Lady Fairburn exclaimed, now getting out of her chair. "Yes, your friend is right, Almeria, for when the time comes for him to reveal himself, you will think him an even more engaging fellow than any other!"

Almeria considered this, aware of the twirling excitement growing steadily within her.

"But I am not pursued by a great many gentlemen as yet. There is no need for him to do so."

"But you *shall* be," her mother declared. "Have you not already received three other bouquets this week? I am certain that more will come in the weeks to follow." The broad smile on her mother's face made Almeria frown, for she was not certain that she found as much delight in it as her mother did. She had always imagined that it would be delightful to be pursued by more than one or two gentlemen, but to be pursued by a gentleman who wished to keep himself anonymous was entirely unexpected. "You shall have to keep a watchful eye whenever you step out into society," her mother instructed, sitting back down and tapping one finger on the arm of her chair to draw Almeria's attention. "This gentleman could be anyone!"

Almeria rolled her eyes, garnering a fierce look from her mother.

"If he could be anyone, then how am I meant to distinguish who he might be."

"I am sure we will find a way." With a slight lift of her chin, her mother smiled indulgently as though Almeria was a child needing encouragement in some small matter. "It will be evident by his way of behaving. No doubt he will seek you out a little more than others might do. You will perhaps catch his eye from across the room, or see something in his smile!"

Almeria wanted to protest that she could not be certain that anyone and everyone who caught her eye was truly interested in her, but wisely chose to remain silent. Her mother was as excited about this as she was. It seemed a little unfair to bring her spirits lower at the moment. Sighing, she spread her hands.

"Very well. I shall be watchful, I promise."

Miss Madeley let out a giggle, one hand pressed to her mouth. When Almeria lifted an eyebrow, her friend dropped her hand.

"I was thinking how well thought out his plan is, for the gentleman has certainly made himself a good deal more amiable to you already, has he not?"

"I do not understand. I—"

"Well," her friend interrupted, sitting forward in her chair, her eyes bright. "You may not even know his name, but already your thoughts are filled with him – and indeed, I am sure you have not even *thought* about any of the other gentlemen who have sent you flowers thus far."

Almeria swallowed, fighting the urge to protest.

"Yes, that is quite so. I had not thought of such a thing."

"Which is why I say he has done very well." Miss Madeley sat back in her chair and tipped her head to one side. "Whoever this is, he has given it a great deal of consideration and managed to garner your attention, without even revealing his name to you! When the time comes for him to do so, he hopes that you will be so delighted to know it, you may immediately feel a deep affection for him."

Almeria shook her head, refuting this immediately.

"I am afraid that I cannot agree with you there. I cannot find myself overly affectionate for any gentleman who keeps himself hidden from me. I may end up knowing his name, but I will know nothing about his character."

Much to her surprise, her mother laughed and threw up her hands, as though Almeria was being ridiculous.

"You may be surprised, my dear." Her mother's lips curved into a knowing smile. "Although you say your feelings will not be at all involved, I am quite of the belief that your feelings will do precisely what you do not wish them to do, in such a case as this."

Almeria did not allow herself to be convinced, however, but let her gaze shift across the room to the tulips which the footman had just set on a side table, in an elegant vase. Whether or not what her mother said was correct, she had to admit that she certainly felt a good deal of interest in this gentleman and the flowers he had sent. Regardless of what else occurred, Almeria was quite sure that her thoughts would be filled with questions over who this gentleman was, and why he had chosen to send her tulips without his name attached to it to them.

A smile touched the corners of her mouth. Whoever this person was, he had done very well, for now her thoughts were filled with none but him.

CHAPTER FOUR

"*A*nd might I sign your dance card?"

Almeria nodded and handed her dance card over to the sixth gentleman who had approached. As the fellow signed it, her eyes caught none other than Lord Coppinger as he made to come towards her. His hands were behind his back, pulling his broad shoulders back a little and the small smile on his face was directed solely at her. Almeria's heart did the most unusual thing, quickening its pace, which was very strange indeed and not a feeling she found particularly pleasant.

Thankfully, Lord Hayling garnered her attention again.

"I have taken the quadrille." Lord Hayling smiled at her as she took the card back from him. "I do hope that is acceptable."

"But of course."

The truth was, she did not want to dance with Lord Hayling, for he was known to be most unsteady when he danced and had trodden on many a young lady's toes.

"I thank you."

He smiled at her, and she almost sighed, when an interruption came in the form of Marcus' voice.

"Am I too late to take any of your dances, Almeria?"

Smiling, she reached out and touched Marcus' arm.

"Certainly not. You know I always have space for you, Marcus." Suddenly aware of Lord Hayling's lifted eyebrow, she coughed lightly. "I should say, Lord Coppinger."

Marcus chuckled and cast a glance at Lord Hayling.

"You need not worry, Lord Hayling. Lady Almeria is not being overfamiliar. Rather, she and I have been as close as brother and sister for many years now."

"I see." Lord Hayling smiled quickly, his look of surprise disappearing. "How very blessed you are to have had such a beauty as Lady Almeria be one of your closest companions. Although," he continued, a slight twinkle in his eye, "I am certain that one day there will be a gentleman who will be able to claim many more years of her company than even you!"

Heat poured into Almeria's face as she darted a glance to Lord Hayling, wondering if he was hoping that he would be such a gentleman. Unfortunately for him, he would *not* be the one she considered, for while he was very amiable, she had not even the smallest flicker of interest in him. Given that she and her friends had promised each other that they would only ever marry for love, there could be no hope for Lord Hayling.

"Of course."

Throwing her a wink, Lord Coppinger smiled briefly and then held out his hand. Quickly, she handed him her dance card, watching as he placed his name down before handing it back to her.

"You did not take my waltz again, I see."

Why was it that she felt so disappointed? It would be

wise not to dance the waltz with the same gentleman twice in a row.

"Alas, I did not ask." Lord Coppinger chuckled. "I did not think it would be fair of me to steal it yet again. I am sure that there are many other gentlemen who would like to garner that privilege for themselves."

Rather astonished with the great swell of dissatisfaction in her heart, Almeria lifted her chin and pushed the feeling away.

"How very gracious of you."

"Is it not?" Lord Coppinger grinned, just as Lord Hayling excused himself, leaving her to stand with Lord Coppinger and her mother nearby. "I should warn you that I have heard that Lord Hayling is very heavy with his feet."

Laughing ruefully, Almeria shook her head and took his arm, finding the warmth of his nearness filling her heart with a gentle sense of contentment.

"Alas, but what is a young lady to do if a gentleman seeks to dance with her? It is very unlikely that she might invent any suitable excuse for why she could not, especially if she wishes to dance with others, but not with him."

Lord Coppinger thought for a moment, then offered her a half-shrug.

"I am afraid I cannot give you an answer." A small smile curved one side of his mouth, giving him an endearing look as he leaned a little toward her. "Though you might simply slip to the powder room during his dance and avoid it altogether – and then pretend to be the most upset, apologetic creature that ever lived when he finds you after the dance ends. I am certain he should forgive you."

Almeria's heart seemed to swell as she smiled up into his face. How well they knew each other! How good it was to be able to laugh and tease one another in such a friendly fashion. With Lord Coppinger, she did not have to be as proper as she ought to be the rest of the time, and even that was something of a relief.

A sudden thought had her smile slipping and instantly, Lord Coppinger looked at her with concern.

"Whatever is the matter?"

Shuddering lightly, Almeria scowled.

"It is not something which I have told you about, as yet, given that I have not seen you, but a gentleman has sent me some bouquets of flowers."

Immediately, Lord Coppinger grinned.

"That does not come as any sort of surprise."

His elbow nudged her gently as Almeria immediately giggled, shaking her head at his teasing.

"You mean to say that you think I should expect to get flowers from many gentlemen," she suggested, seeing his grey eyes alight with mirth. "Very well. While you are very kind to suggest so, there is something unusual about two of the bouquets which I have received thus far." Lord Coppinger said nothing, waiting for her to finish her explanation, and Almeria continued with relish. "Thus far of the bouquets which I have received, two have had no note attached. Therefore, whoever has sent them has kept his name from me." To her surprise, Lord Coppinger did not appear to be in any way surprised at this. He did not frown. He did not even lift his eyebrows towards his hairline. Rather, he merely nodded as if such a thing was to be expected. "You have perhaps heard of gentlemen doing such a thing as this already, I think?"

He shook his head.

"No... I was merely thinking about why a gentleman might do such a thing. It could be that the note was lost on the way, could it not?"

Almeria shrugged.

"Mayhap, but both bouquets have been of tulips, and neither have had a note. My friends and my mother think it is deliberate."

A chuckle broke from his lips, making Almeria frown.

"Now I know why you appeared concerned – it is because you fear that it is Lord Hayling who is sending those flowers to you, do you not?"

Her eyebrows lifting, Almeria leaned into him.

"How is it that you know me so well, Marcus?" she asked, lapsing back into that old familiarity. "Yes, indeed. I fear very much that Lord Hayling is the gentleman who has sent me those flowers. If it is him, then what shall I do?"

"I think that you give Lord Hayling a little too much credit." Seeing her open her mouth to ask what he meant, Lord Coppinger quickly began to explain. "To send flowers without a note with a particular reason in mind would require a good deal of thought and consideration. I believe that is something which Lord Hayling lacks the capacity for, I am afraid."

Letting out a small gasp, the corner of her mouth lifting just a little, Almeria loosened her grip on Lord Coppinger's arm.

"Good gracious, Lord Coppinger. Are you truly attempting to tell me that Lord Hayling lacks good sense? That he is not the wisest of gentlemen?"

Lord Coppinger immediately began to stutter, only for him to roll his eyes and chuckle when he realized that she had been teasing him, for Almeria could not keep her grin hidden.

"You are already aware of Lord Hayling's reputation, then?"

"I am." With a shrug of her shoulders, she looked out

across the dance floor. "You said that he is not the wisest of fellows but that, to me, does still suggest that he might have sent such flowers. He could have simply forgotten to write a note." She caught her breath, her eyes widening suddenly. "Mayhap he forgot that he already sent me one bouquet, and thereafter sent me another!"

Lord Coppinger laughed and put his other hand on her arm for a moment in a comforting gesture, turning himself towards her a little more.

"Mayhap, but I believe it is highly unlikely. Lord Hayling has not shown any particular preference to you as yet, has he?" Biting her lip, Almeria shook her head, realizing slowly that she wanted this unknown gentleman to be someone of worth. She certainly did not want it to be someone akin to Lord Hayling! "Besides which, Lord Hayling is a gentleman who flits from one lady to the next. He would not have given any thought to the sort of flowers that he might send to a lady such as yourself, for tulips have significance, do they not?" Tsking lightly, he shook his head. "I am sure he was not the one who sent them to you."

Her fears slowly subsided, and Almeria let out a long breath.

"Might I ask – do most gentlemen of the *ton* know the meaning behind the different flowers they might send to a lady?"

"I should hope so!" Lord Coppinger exclaimed, his eyes dancing. "Save for the gentlemen such as Lord Hayling, however."

Considering this, Almeria nodded slowly.

"As I have said, I was sent a bouquet of tulips, which I believe symbolize friendship but given they were purple also, I was told it speaks of an appreciation of me." Disliking the fact that she was speaking of herself in such a way, she took a breath. "Whoever this gentleman is, mayhap he was acquainted with me last Season. I suppose that cannot be said of Lord Hayling."

"Indeed." Lord Coppinger smiled and squeezed her arm again. "You do appear to be rather taken with this puzzle, I must say."

Almeria tossed up one hand.

"Well, would you not be also?" she demanded. "If you were sent two very beautiful arrangements of flowers, without a note telling you who had sent them, would it not be on your mind? Would you not be looking around the room, even at this very moment, wondering which gentleman might have sent them?" Seeing him grin, a blush rose on her cheeks. "Very well, you may tease me, knowing that gentlemen would not often be sent flowers, but all the same, it is very mysterious, and it certainly *has* caught my attention."

"Which must be the very intention of the fellow who sent them to you."

Twisting her head, Almeria looked at him sharply.

"That is precisely what Miss Madeley said also," she murmured quietly. "Which is another reason for it not to have been Lord Hayling. I was foolish to be concerned." Lord Coppinger snorted and Almeria's lips curved, and she laughed with him. As she did so, the sense of contentment which came with simply being in his company became all-encompassing. It filled her right through and she leaned more closely against him, glad that they were back amongst the shadows of the room, a little hidden from the prying eyes of others. "There is something else I might do." Considering aloud, she tipped her head. "Lady Yardley, as you know, has 'The London Ledger'." She lifted one shoulder as Lord Coppinger's smile suddenly cracked.

"Mayhap I might use it to beg whoever has sent me these flowers to come and reveal their name to me."

Lord Coppinger frowned, his grey eyes now a little set.

"Is there such a need for that as yet? You have only had two bouquets so far. Who is to say whether there shall be more?" Slowly, Almeria nodded, catching the edge of her lip between her teeth. Had she been overly confident about this? "And even if more flowers arrived, would it be wise to let all of society know? You know how society delights to talk and whisper." He pulled his arm away from hers gently but smiled as he did so. "Even now I can see that Lady White has been watching us for some minutes, which is why I must now stand away from you."

A small sigh escaped her, seeing precisely what he meant by such warnings.

"I should not want to become the object of society's attention, certainly."

"Then do be cautious," Lord Coppinger replied softly. "Whoever this gentleman is, I am sure that he will reveal himself to you in time." One shoulder lifted as his lips curved into a smile. "After all, your mother, Miss Madeley, and I think that he is doing this to gain your attention, to have you think on him and wonder about him. No doubt he will inform you precisely as to who he is when he thinks that the time is right, in the hope that you will be overjoyed to finally learn his name."

Almeria immediately let out a loud groan, which brought a look of genuine surprise to Lord Coppinger's face. When she rolled her eyes and tipped her head to the left, his look of astonishment was replaced with a grin as he realized who was now approaching.

"It seems it is time for me to step away," he murmured

as Almeria groaned again. "Hush!" Grinning, he leaned closer. "He will hear you!"

Inclining his head in farewell, Lord Coppinger stepped away and Almeria allowed her eyes to follow him for a short while. There was something different about Lord Coppinger. Yes, she was content in his company, and yes, she often had very enjoyable conversations with him, but there was something more to their connection now, something deeper.

She did not have time to wonder about what it was, however, for Lord Hayling came directly towards her, inclined his head, and then offered her his arm.

"It is time for us to dance, Lady Almeria!"

"So it is." Silently praying that he would not stand on her feet, Almeria stepped out to the dance floor on Lord Hayling's arm – but her thoughts were not focused on him. Instead, she found herself searching out Lord Coppinger as she walked, thinking on the strange, lingering awareness of him, questions continuing to rise in her mind.

What was it about him that had changed?

CHAPTER FIVE

*M*arcus smiled as Lord Trevelyan came to sit down beside him.

"Good afternoon, old friend."

"Good afternoon."

Lord Trevelyan lifted an eyebrow.

"So how does your little plan go at present?"

"You mean with Lady Almeria?" Lord Trevelyan sighed, looking straight back at him as Marcus chuckled. "Very well, I shall tell you." Sitting back in his chair, he spread out both hands. "Thus far I have sent three bouquets, with a fourth planned for tomorrow. I think I might add roses to it very soon."

His friend nodded, smiling lightly.

"It is going very well, then."

Considering for a moment, Marcus lifted his shoulders.

"It is very hard to say, given that I do not know what Lady Almeria is thinking. She may have given up trying to work out who it is already."

His friend let out a bark of laughter, wiggling one finger in Marcus' direction.

"That I do *not* believe, given the brightness in your eyes. You were speaking to her of the bouquets, were you not? I saw you in deep conversation some nights ago, I am sure."

"I am often in deep conversation with Almeria," Marcus protested, but he could not keep the grin from spreading across his face. "Very well. I will admit to you that I spoke to Lady Almeria about the flowers, although she was the one who brought them into the discussion in the first place. From what I understand, she is highly intrigued as to who has sent them to her – though I cannot say whether she still feels that way."

"Then when will you tell her all?" Marcus' smile spiraled away from his face. He had been so busy sending bouquets of flowers that he had not given a single thought to when he would confess. "You do not know?" Hearing the incredulous tone of his friend's voice, Marcus rolled his eyes and scowled. "Surely you must tell her soon. What happens if some other gentleman snatches her away? You must not delay too long. She will grow tired of the mystery otherwise."

Taking a deep breath, Marcus thought about this for a moment, then nodded.

"I shall tell her within a fortnight."

He nearly swore aloud as his friend tilted his head, his brows lifting as if he were considering whether or not this was too great a length of time.

"Let us hope that she is not persuaded to be courted by another fellow while you wait to reveal your heart."

This thought was almost too worrisome for words, and Marcus looked away, reaching for his brandy and taking a sip so that he might bring a little warmth back into his chest. He had been pleased by how Almeria had spoken of the bouquets he had sent thus far, delighting in her questions and her wonderings, and finding his heart leaping at the thought of how much joy his flowers had brought her. Now, however, he realized that he needed to consider what he would do next. Almeria would have to know about his flowers, and therefore, his feelings, very soon. If he did not tell her, then what Lord Trevallyan had suggested might actually happen, and that was a serious thought indeed.

"I shall have roses added to the next bouquet." Lord Trevelyan frowned and opened his mouth, but then shook his head, saying nothing. Mayhap he thought that Marcus should have added roses to his flowers already, but Marcus had not yet felt ready. He had not wanted to rush the situation with Almeria and thus had been very careful indeed. Perhaps, he considered, a little too careful. "If you will excuse me, I must be going."

Getting to his feet, he caught his friend's look of surprise.

"Wherever are you going in such a rush?"

"To act on your advice!" Marcus responded. "I must go at once to the shop and have roses added to the next bouquet. I cannot delay even a moment longer!"

"I confess I was quite delighted when you agreed to walk with me this afternoon." Marcus' heart had lurched when Almeria had warmly agreed to walk with him in St James Park. She had seen it as nothing more than walking with a friend, of course, while he was overwhelmed with such a great sense of delight, it was difficult not to allow it to express itself in his features. "There is so much I must learn about you and you about I." Lady Almeria slipped her arm through his and, quite unexpectedly, a great and overwhelming heat flooded Marcus' frame. "We have been so many years apart, and while our letters have been numerous, I confess I have made them a little less frequent of late."

"I shall not hold that against you." Laughing at her wry grin, Marcus smiled at her, thinking how beautiful she was with her swirling hazel eyes smiling back at him. Did she know how much she offered him when she bestowed her smile upon him? "Tell me, how does it go with your estate? I understand that you had a good many responsibilities to assume when you first took on the title - as well as enduring your year of mourning. I am assuming that you miss your father a great deal."

Marcus nodded slowly.

"I do, certainly, for he was a wise man. However, in his later years, he did not take as much care of the estate as he ought to have. I now find myself with a little more responsibility than I had at first anticipated, for it has taken the last two summers to bring the estate back to its full potential. Thankfully, the crops are flourishing, my tenants are happy, and all is now well."

"You were always a very responsible and considerate sort. I am sure that your father would be very proud of you."

Something tight grew in Marcus' chest and he paused in their conversation for a moment, unable to speak, such was the great sense of loss that washed through him again. His father had been the only parent he had ever known, and they had shared a great bond, a deep connection which had been a great loss to him when the time came for it to be severed.

"My father always made certain to take his responsibilities with all seriousness, and I intend to do the same. I will not allow my family name to be lost, which is why you find me now here in London."

"Ah yes, I had quite forgotten you were intending to find yourself a bride this Season." Suddenly there was no longer a smile on Lady Almeria's face. Instead, she turned her head, looking away from him as if she wanted to hide her expression. "And have you had any success in that regard?"

Marcus cleared his throat, uncertain as to why there had come a strange tension between them.

"No, I have not, but I have not been particularly specific in my search as yet. It will come in time, I am sure."

"In time?" Lady Almeria laughed suddenly and shook her head. "I think you will find yourself without a bride, come the end of the Season, if you continue to believe that you have time to be tardy! Does not a young lady require a time of interest, where walks are taken and cups of tea shared? *Then* comes courtship and after that, a betrothal - provided that you are both as contented with one another as you believe." Marcus was about to say that he had no requirement for such a thing, given that his heart was already committed to hers, but he chose instead to remain quiet. Now was not the time to declare himself, but all the same, it took great strength for him not to speak a word. He remained silent for so long that Lady Almeria stopped walking, turning to face him a little more, her fingers now curling around his wrist. "I do hope I did not insult you."

"No, not in the least." Reassuring her quickly, he smiled. "It is only that I find myself considering what you said. You are quite right, mayhap I should make a good deal more of my current situation and act with greater haste. I must think about what I ought to do."

They walked in silence for a few moments. Lady Almeria broke the quiet. Her voice was a little strained this time, with a slight catch in her throat as she was not quite certain that she wanted to ask the question she spoke.

"Might I ask if you have an interest in any particular young lady as yet?"

Drawing a great breath of air into his lungs, Marcus licked his lips before he answered.

Should I tell her now?

"I certainly have consideration," he replied quietly. "I will not pretend that I have no interest in anyone. I confess, in fact, I have a somewhat *fixed* interest, but whether or not I will permit myself to pursue it, I am not certain as yet."

"Oh."

Her voice was very small, and she turned her head away again, so that the bonnet hid her features from him. Marcus could not quite understand her reaction, having expected her to be either interested or pleased to hear that he had such feelings. Again, silence came between them. It was almost an unnatural silence – not one he enjoyed, and certainly not akin to any previous ones which they had shared. There was a hint of strain, as though a wall had built itself between them, hiding them each from the other's view.

I should ask her the same.

Tension coiled in his stomach as the words came to his lips, pushing themselves forward until finally, they made their way to Lady Almeria's ears.

"And have you any gentlemen of interest as yet? I see you very often surrounded by gentlemen during balls and soirees and the like. I am sure that some of them are very eager for your company!"

Lady Almeria chuckled softly and looked back at him.

"Alas, whilst such a thing may be true, there are a good many of them akin to Lord Hayling, and quite frankly, I do not wish for them to prolong their time in my company." Thankfully, her laughter pushed away the strain between them, which faded, and a companionable silence returned to take its place. "Although I will confess that there is one gentleman who has been showing me a little more attention than others lately."

Having never expected to hear such a thing from her, Marcus sucked in a breath.

"Oh." Coughing, he lifted his chin. "Is he an honorable gentleman?" Trying to smile, he nudged her lightly. "Or is he a gentleman you wish to ignore entirely?"

A large part of him prayed it would be the latter, only for his hopes to be dashed as she laughed.

"It is Lord Penforth." Her eyebrows lifted as she looked at him. "From your response, I would say that you have not heard much about him! I hope that means there is nothing but good things said about his reputation and character."

Urgently Marcus searched his mind for anything which might be wrong with Lord Penforth, but he could recall little. No, he considered, there was nothing the gentleman had done or said which would make society turn against him. A trifle irritated, he still managed to smile, although it faded very quickly.

"From what I know, Lord Penforth is a genial fellow, albeit a quiet one."

She laughed brightly.

"I certainly shall not hold that against him," she remarked, grinning. "If he is a fine fellow, then I shall give him the opportunity to steal my heart."

Marcus' heart pulsed with a snap of pain as he looked at her sharply.

"I beg your pardon?"

THE EARL'S UNSPOKEN LOVE | 47

Lady Almeria blushed beautifully, looking at him for a long moment before, with a sigh, she continued.

"No doubt you will think me a little foolish, but I have every intention of making myself fall in love. I wish very much to be in love, and therefore have decided I shall *only* marry a gentleman who has cause to love me – and who I have fallen in love with."

Her chin lifted, her eyes flashing as though she dared him to refute her idea.

Stopping their walk, Marcus turned to her, casting a quick glance over her shoulder and seeing Lady Fairburn no longer watching them, but now in deep conversation with a friend. Looking back at Lady Almeria, Marcus swallowed hard. His breath was coming so quickly that he feared it might pull the words from his lips before he was ready but, inwardly, he was practically dancing with both joy and terror. This was his moment. *This* was the time he would tell her the truth of his heart.

I love you, he wanted to say. *I shall always love you. If only you will give me an opportunity, I shall give you all of myself.*

He grasped her hand, a little overwhelmed at the opportunity which had been given him.

"Oh, my dear Almeria." His heart was beating painfully, and he took a breath, hearing a roaring in his ears. "I do not think it foolish, not in the least." Closing his eyes, he lifted his chin and looked down into her beautiful face, seeing how her hazel eyes searched his. "There is something I must tell you. I –"

"I am so *very* sorry to interrupt."

Marcus stammered to a stop, but quickly dropped Almeria's hand, not wanting anyone to see their close connection. Turning, he forced a smile in Lord Penforth's direction, battling his anger at being so interrupted.

Lord Penforth smiled genially back, though his gaze was fixed on Lady Almeria. He was a tall, rather slim man with a crop of thick golden hair and piercing blue eyes which, to Marcus' mind always appeared to be somewhat cold. But then again, he considered, a little ashamed of himself, was he not thinking such a thing simply because of this interruption?

"Again, I am sorry to interrupt, but I could not simply walk past you without greeting you."

Fully aware that Lord Penforth's attention was turned solely to Lady Almeria rather than to himself, Marcus cleared his throat and finally caught a look from Lord Penforth.

"But of course." he managed to say in a calm tone, as Lady Almeria inclined her head. "You have thought to take the afternoon air also, I see."

Lord Penforth did not respond to Marcus, looking only at Lady Almeria as though she were the morning sun that brought the day into all of its glory. Marcus could not blame him for it. Lady Almeria held such beauty – both of face and character – that he had always believed no one could compare to her.

Desperately, he wished that there was something untoward about Lord Penforth's character, something which would push him away from Lady Almeria, but in his heart, he knew there was not. He did not know the fellow particularly well, but a man's reputation could easily be sullied, and all of society would know of it. Even though Marcus had not been in London all that often, he was certain that he would have heard a whisper of any wrongdoing on Lord Penforth's part.

"Will you be at the ball this evening?" Lord Penforth smiled warmly at Lady Almeria, a hopeful glint coming into his eye, and Marcus' stomach dropped.

"Yes, I have every intention of attending."

"I do hope you will permit me to dance with you, for it has been some time since I have been able to do so, has it not?"

Lady Almeria's tinkling laugh shattered Marcus' heart.

She seems so at ease with him. Might she be considering him as a potential suitor?

"Good gracious, Lord Penforth, we have not danced together for only two days. I hardly think that is an excessive amount of time."

Lord Penforth sighed and shook his head.

"Ah, is it only as short a time as that? Well, it must be simply because I am so very eager to dance with you that it appears so pronounced! Perhaps it is a recognition of how much I desire your very fine company."

Marcus shot Lady Almeria a glance, seeing how easily she smiled at Lord Penforth. He was nothing to either of them at this present moment, he realized; naught but a shadow – present but unacknowledged.

What happens if some other gentleman snatches her away? You must not delay too long.

Lord Trevelyan's words came back to his mind as Marcus lowered his head, taking a long breath. Was this the beginning of such a thing? Had Lord Trevelyan spoken the future without being aware of it?

After a few more minutes of general conversation, Lord Penforth took his leave, barely glancing at Marcus before he inclined his head and stepped away. To Marcus' utter dismay, Lady Almeria let out a soft sigh, a smile on her face as her gaze followed the gentleman.

"I am quite certain that I could fall in love with him," she declared firmly, turning her head away to look up at Marcus. "Do you not think so? He is a very handsome gentleman and quite amiable. Do you think that he has the potential to care for me?"

"I think anyone has the potential to care for you, Almeria," Marcus spoke from his heart, feeling it break into tiny fragments as she turned to face him, her eyes seeming to glow with a new sense of evident happiness. "You are a wonderful young lady. Any gentleman who manages to steal your heart will be the most fortunate of fellows."

She tilted her head at him and smiled.

"You do say the kindest things, Marcus." Slipping one hand through his arm, she began to walk again, and Marcus had no other choice but to fall into step beside her, wishing Lord Penforth had interrupted them only a few moments later, so that Marcus might have had the opportunity to tell Lady Almeria the truth about how he felt. Yes, he might do so now – but Almeria's thoughts were on Lord Penforth at present. The idea of speaking of his own heart now seemed a little foolish. "Wait!" Lady Almeria's voice was suddenly very excited indeed. "What if *he* is the one who has been sending me the bouquets? What if this is his way of encouraging my attentions?"

Marcus had not thought that he could experience more pain than having a shattered heart, only for yet another moment of jarring agony to blast its way through him.

"You should ask him." It was the only thing he could think to say, for if she did ask Lord Penforth and he made it clear that he had very little idea of what she spoke of, then no doubt, she would wonder who else it was sending her flowers. Perhaps then he might find himself with a little more hope. "Yes, I think you should simply ask him."

Lady Almeria giggled.

"Sometimes I think that you are just as eager to find out the truth as I am, Marcus." Smiling, she looked up at him again. "You are the most wonderful friend. I hope you know how glad I am that you are here this Season. It has been a joy to my heart to be in company with you again."

Marcus' throat constricted.

"As joyful as I am to be with you again also, Almeria," he managed to say, wishing she could see into the depths of his heart and know just how much he truly felt for her. "My life was not the same without your presence."

Her smile softened and she leaned into him a little more.

"I feel the very same," she murmured quietly, and Marcus' heart cried out in agony all over again.

CHAPTER SIX

"*I* think I should like to put something into 'The London Ledger'."

Her words drew a few audible gasps from her friends, for both married and unmarried were sitting together, taking tea in Lady Yardley's drawing room. Lord Yardley had gone out this afternoon, leaving the ladies to themselves.

"How very interesting." Lady Yardley smiled warmly. "And what is it you intend to put in 'The London Ledger'?"

Almeria spread her hands.

"It is about all the bouquets I have been receiving."

Her friends either nodded or cast her an assured glance, for they all knew that she had been receiving bouquets without notes attached every two or three days, and another had arrived only that afternoon.

"You want to find out who has been sending them?"

Almeria nodded in answer to Lady Sherbourne's question.

"I confess it has been both exciting and a little frustrating to know that someone is eager for my prolonged company, but as yet has not revealed themself."

"I can understand that." As the others nodded, Lady Sherbourne continued. "Then you are determined to take this situation into your own hands?"

Almeria smiled.

"Yes, I think so, although he very well still may choose not to tell me! At least then I make it clear that I am eager to find out his identity."

"I think that's a very charming idea," Lady Yardley smiled. "Might I be so bold as to ask you – and pray forgive me for asking in public – whether or not you have considered that the sender might be Lord Penforth?"

A soft heat rose in Almeria's face as her other friends looked at her; some with lifted eyebrows and some smiling quietly.

"I – I am sure you will all be aware that Lord Penforth has been a little more interested in my company of late."

"Lord Penforth is a very reputable gentleman, from what I believe." Miss Millington remarked as Lady Yardley nodded. "You think that he is the one who has been sending you flowers?"

Almeria shrugged.

"If he is, he has not revealed himself to me as yet." Her shoulders dropped. "That is why, if it *is* he, then I would like to hear it from him."

"And if he is not the one sending the flowers?"

Lady Elizabeth lifted her eyebrows, waiting, and Almeria could only shrug.

"If it is Lord Penforth, then all is well. It is *not* that I would then decide against Lord Penforth in favor of whichever gentleman is sending me these flowers," she protested, although her voice, even to her, sounded a little weak. "But I would perhaps be a little more restrained in my forwardness, should I know that there is another gentleman eager to seek me out. I should like to know who it is, at the very least."

From the smiles on every face, it was clear that her friends all understood precisely what it was she was feeling.

"I think it very romantic indeed." Miss Millington sighed, one hand pressed lightly at her heart. "He is a mysterious gentleman for certain, one who has thought carefully about what he will do to garner your attention."

"And it has worked exceedingly well," Lady Elizabeth added as everyone else nodded. "I think we are all agog to discover who the sender is."

Lady Yardley laughed but then turned to Almeria with a look of interest.

"I understand that your last bouquet was a little different from the previous ones."

"It was." Seeing that her friends were all now looking at her, listening to every word she had to say, Almeria smiled. "There were roses within it."

In an instant, gasps lifted from almost everyone, with some of them pressing their hands to their mouths, clearly aware of the significance of the roses.

"First, purple tulips to show affection and admiration," Lady Landon murmured softly. "And then roses to signify that the affection has turned to love."

Hearing her friend speak such a thing, Lady Almeria's heart began to press hard against her chest, her pulse quickening and her face heating a little. She bit the edge of her lip, uncertain as to whether or not to agree with what her friend had said, only to see everyone else nodding.

"But there is still a warning," Lady Yardley interrupted

gently. "The reason I say such a thing to you– aside from Lady Landon and Lady Sherbourne – is to make it plain that just because a gentleman declares that he is in love with you does not mean that you must therefore give your heart to him in return. There is no obligation there."

Lady Sherbourne – who had been Lady Cassandra and was the cousin of Lady Yardley, nodded fervently, leading forward little in her chair.

"I certainly should say so. You know we have all agreed to marry for love, and both Lady Landon and I have been very blessed in finding our husbands, but for my part, it would not have been a suitable match had I rushed into an attachment without first acknowledging my feelings."

Lady Landon nodded.

"I would agree. Whenever a gentleman declares himself or even shows you the beginnings of an interest, you ought to examine your own heart to be certain there is a genuine feeling within you also. Lord Landon and I care for each other so very much and that, I am sure, is what makes our marriage so very contented. To find that you do not love the person you have wed only a short time after your marriage has taken place must be deeply distressing."

Almeria licked her lips, considering this. While she was not in danger of giving her heart to a gentleman she did not know, the possibility was there still. She ought not to let her thoughts continually be on this mysterious gentleman until she knew for certain who he was.

"Besides which, whoever the gentleman is, he might be the most unhandsome of fellows," Miss Millington inter-jected and Almeria immediately laughed, the tension pushing away from her. "Or he may be one who treads on your toes during the dance, or holds you far too close when you waltz, or whose breath is most unbecoming – or indeed, someone who has already found himself a wife."

With so much laughter running around the room, Almeria found herself smiling, sitting back in her chair with her shoulders relaxing.

"And what of Lord Coppinger?"

In one moment it was as if all of the laughter had been pulled out of the room. Almeria suddenly went cold, her skin tingling as she turned her head to see Lady Yardley's questioning look.

"Forgive me, I do not know what you mean."

Lady Yardley laughed lightly, reached across, and put a hand on Almeria's arm for a moment.

"Forgive me, that was a little abrupt. In all of the excitement you have quite forgotten - do you recall saying that you would introduce your friends to Lord Coppinger? Might I ask if you have done so as yet? There is only Lady Elizabeth, Miss Millington, and Miss Madeley. Since all of them seek a match with a gentleman willing to fall in love with them and since you have said repeatedly how excellent a fellow Lord Coppinger is, it seems to make perfect sense to introduce them all. That is, so long as he is open to the notion of being in love!"

As a murmur ran around the room, Almeria swallowed tightly, wishing she could force a smile, but finding the effort much too difficult.

"I have already introduced him to Lady Elizabeth and Miss Millington." Seeing her friends nod, she looked to Miss Madeley whose gaze was settled on her folded hands in her lap. "Alas, as yet, I have not yet introduced him to Miss Madeley. I have every intention of doing so, of course, as soon as there is an appropriate time."

Lady Yardley nodded, seeming pleased.

"Thank you, it would be good if he could steal the heart of one of your friends, would it not? He appears to be quite eager for a bride, given the many young ladies he has danced with on these last few occasions."

Saying nothing, Almeria nodded, choosing not to reveal that Lord Coppinger was, in fact, seeking to wed. Why was it that, whenever Lord Coppinger was mentioned, she seemed to react so strangely? It was most irregular. It was as though she did not want him to be wed, as though she did not want him to find a wife, nor to fall in love with any one of her friends - but why such a thing should be, she could not imagine! Her face flushed warm as she dropped her gaze, certain that, if her friends or Lady Yardley could read her thoughts at present, their opinion of her would drop significantly.

"Lord Coppinger, from what I understand, is an excellent fellow," Lady Yardley continued, speaking to the room as Almeria's jaw tightened, her hands curling into gentle fists. "Lady Almeria has known him for such a long time, and says wonderful things about him - and indeed, as I have moved about society, I find that not a bad word has been said about him. I think he is a very rare sort of gentleman, who makes certain to behave correctly in all things and without the smallest hint of impropriety in any matter whatsoever." Her smile again alighted upon Almeria. "Would you concur, Lady Almeria?"

Not trusting her voice, Almeria nodded and again tried to smile, but her lips refused to remove themselves from the tight line they had formed. Why was it that her chest was so tight, her skin so very prickly? There was no explanation for this particular emotion, for Lord Coppinger had made himself quite clear he was seeking a bride. She ought to be doing everything she could to encourage him to find a suitable match, especially if it could be with one of her friends. Why then did she find herself so restrained?

"I should very much like to be introduced to him, then."

The hopeful glint in Miss Madeley's eye made Almeria's reluctance only grow, though she did not say anything akin to what she felt.

"Yes, of course. He is an outstanding gentleman, and I am only sorry that I have not yet had the opportunity to introduce you to him."

She fought to smile, but then fell silent, praying that she would not be asked any further questions about Lord Coppinger. Perhaps it was because they had not seen each other for so many years that she was a little uncomfortable in encouraging him toward one of her friends. Yes, she considered, looking down at her tightly laced fingers in her lap, that *had* to be the reason, for there was no other explanation she could find.

"Very well then." Lady Yardley smiled happily. "For you, Lady Almeria, I shall have something written in 'The London Ledger' for tomorrow, and you might look for an opportunity to introduce Lord Coppinger to Miss Madeley."

"Yes. I shall."

Almeria kept her head lowered, her tone low, while her heart thudded dully.

"And let us hope that Lord Penforth is the gentleman who has been sending you these flowers!" Lady Elizabeth laughed as Almeria looked up at her friend. "For that would make you very contented indeed, I am sure."

Again, Almeria tried to smile, but it simply would not come. Her confusion over her feelings grew all the more for suddenly, her interest in Lord Penforth seemed to have waned. In fact, she couldn't recall what she found attractive about him. Wishing she could have a little silence to allow her thoughts to regulate themselves, Almeria took a breath and closed her eyes for a moment. Thankfully, Lady Yardley soon began to discuss another matter and Almeria was left to sit alone, doing her very best not to think of Lord Coppinger.

CHAPTER SEVEN

"*H*as anyone approached you yet?"

Almeria shook her head.

Her nerves were twisting like writhing snakes, and she could not seem to hold any gentleman's gaze for more than a brief moment. Lady Yardley had included a short article in 'The London Ledger', stating she had become aware that a young lady by the name of Lady Almeria had been sent many bouquets of flowers, but without a gentleman claiming to have done so. There had been a short paragraph with a few other details, ending with the statement that she knew, of a certainty, that Lady Almeria was eager to know the name of the mysterious and intriguing gentleman who sent her such gifts.

That edition had been handed out in society the previous day but, as yet, no one had come near her. Almeria did not know whether she was nervous or relieved, for if no one came forward, then mayhap it had just been that the notes had been lost. Perhaps then she might consider Lord Penforth entirely and forget about the whole situation... but if someone did draw near, if someone else declared themselves, then she would have a good deal more to contend with.

"This is the second social occasion I have attended since 'The London Ledger' was printed yesterday." She swallowed at the tightness which balled in her throat, looking to Miss Madeley, who smiled sympathetically, clearly aware of the strain Almeria was under at present. "Every time I have drawn myself into conversation with a gentleman, I have been silently waiting for them to declare themselves!" Hearing those words coming from her mouth, she laughed ruefully and passed one hand over her eyes, quite certain she sounded ridiculous. "I believe myself to be quite foolish of course, but you will understand my situation. I confess I find it quite untenable!"

"I do not understand fully, but I can sympathize with you, certainly." Miss Madeley smiled sweetly and looped her arm through Almeria's. "Come, take a turn around the room with me and I am sure that it will help you feel a little better."

With a nod, Almeria allowed her friend to lead her away, though she could not keep her eyes from catching on almost every gentleman they passed, mentally questioning herself about every one of them. Was that gentleman the one who had sent her the flowers? Was *this* the one who secretly admired her? Was *he* to be the one who would declare himself? She did not hear her friend's conversation, did not listen to a word that was spoken to her, and it was not until they had done one full lap of the room that she finally came back to herself. Realizing that Miss Madeley had spoken for a good length of time, but she had heard none of it, Almeria was about to apologize, only for her friend to simply smile, appearing unaware or unconcerned over Almeria's lack of attention.

"Now, do you feel any better?"

Taking a deep breath, Almeria hesitated, finding her thoughts to be just as jumbled as before, but at the same time, having no wish to disappoint her friend.

"I must be a little less concerned," she answered, managing a smile. "My heart is not pounding as quickly as it was before."

Her mind was still a knot of questions and wonderings, but she did not say such a thing to Miss Madeley.

"Well, that is certainly a good sign." Miss Madeley smiled encouragingly. "Should you like to take another short walk? I am sure that you will feel even better thereafter. Mayhap we might ask your mother to accompany us out of doors? The French doors are open and the evening is pleasant enough for us to step outside without becoming chilled, I am sure."

Almeria took in a deep breath, considering the idea, but then choosing to remain indoors.

"It is a kind suggestion, but I am due to dance very soon. I do not think I should stray too far away, for fear that he will come looking for me and will find me absent." She managed a quiet laugh. "And what if *he* is the one who has been sending me bouquets? I should appear very rude indeed, should I not? And perhaps then I might lose his gifts and his consideration for good!"

Smiling, Miss Madeley tilted her head, looking at her.

"And who are you to dance with?"

Quickly, Almeria checked her dance card.

"It is with Lord Jefferies." She shook her head as Miss Madeley smiled. "He is not the best of dancers. Mayhap I should hope it is *not* he who has sent me the flowers."

"No, he is not."

Miss Madeley chuckled softly, but Almeria only

managed a slight smile, her laugher choked away by her ongoing concern. Seeing her friend's lifted eyebrow, she spread her hands.

"I had not expected this. I did not think I would feel such great anxiety once I had asked Lady Yardley to write about this in the 'The London Ledger'. I believe I considered that quite the opposite would happen."

"You thought you would feel a good deal more at ease."

Almeria nodded.

"Mayhap that was foolish, but that was my expectation. Now, however, I find my anxiety has risen to such a great level that I can barely contain myself."

Miss Madeley put a comforting hand on Almeria's arm, her eyes shining with evident sympathy.

"I understand. There was no need for you to be nervous beforehand, for you had no knowledge of when he would choose to reveal himself to you. Now, however, you are in eager expectation of the gentleman, waiting for him to reveal himself to you very soon, and I can imagine that the wait is not a pleasant one." She shrugged. "After all, what if he is a disgraceful fellow? What if he is unkind? Or worst of all, what if he is ugly?!"

The latter suggestion was so surprising, Almeria could not help but laugh and as she did so, some of her worry flew away with the sound. Catching her breath, she shook her head, still smiling and seeing Miss Madeley grin.

"That would be a very great concern indeed, I am sure. I certainly would *not* be able to consider him."

Miss Madeley chuckled.

"For we all know that you must fall in love with a very handsome gentleman indeed." Her eyebrow lifted. "Lord Coppinger is a handsome fellow, I think. Thank you for introducing me last evening."

Instantly the smile on Almeria's face faded.

"Yes, I suppose he is."

It came as a twist to her stomach to hear her friend say such a thing about Lord Coppinger, which was even more strange.

"I do not think that you like me saying such a thing as that." Clearly observant, Miss Madeley twisted her head, speaking quite plainly. "Is it because you are concerned that I would not be a good match for him?" Almeria swallowed hard, instantly picturing Miss Madeley and Lord Coppinger standing up together at the front of the church while she sat in the pews, watching them. A cold bead of sweat trickled down her back. "Goodness, you need not look so upset at the thought!" Miss Madeley laughed and squeezed Almeria's hand, who quickly flushed with embarrassment. "I have no intention of pursuing him if that is what you are worried about. It does not stop me from thinking him handsome, however."

Silently praying that she could smile, Almeria waited for a moment, but the expression would not come. Seeing Miss Madeley's questioning look, she shook her head.

"He is my dear friend," she said by way of explanation. "I am simply concerned that he will not find the very best partner for himself, and thus be miserable... though that is not to say that I do not think you suitable. Of course you are."

Speaking hastily, she dropped her head with a groan as Miss Madeley chuckled.

"I am glad you think so." She tilted her head. "I have heard that he has been seen stepping out with Miss Tennant. Do you think *her* suitable?"

This was said in a teasing manner, but all the same, Almeria found herself frowning.

"It is not my place to say whether or not anyone attentive to Lord Coppinger would be a suitable match, I suppose," she answered, even though hearing such words made her stomach tense. "Despite my concern, I am certain that he is more than able to decipher such things for himself."

"A very careful answer, I think." Miss Madeley smiled gently. "You say that you have been friends for a long time?"

"Since we were children." Almeria sighed quietly, thinking back to the many years she had spent in his company. "I consider us to be more family than anything else which, of course, will explain why I am so very concerned."

"Indeed. I am sure that you were concerned for your own siblings when it came to their matches," Miss Madeley murmured, turning her head away to look around the room. This remark had Almeria's stomach twisting again, for the truth was that, at the time, she had shown very little interest in whom her siblings had wed. As long as her parents had thought them suitable, that was all that mattered. So why then was she so concerned for Lord Coppinger?

"Ah, good evening! We were just speaking of you!"

Much to Almeria's horror, Miss Madeley's words were directed to none other than Lord Coppinger himself. He looked at Miss Madeley and then to Almeria, before inclining his head.

"Oh?"

"It was nothing of significance." Almeria waved one hand. "Miss Madeley was just telling me about Miss Tennant."

Lord Coppinger blinked.

"Miss Tennant?"

"Yes, or whoever it is you have been stepping out with recently."

Her words were tight and short as she saw Lord Coppinger's eyebrows lift, filling her with acute embarrassment. Why was she speaking so? Why was she behaving in such a fashion? This was her friend. She had no reason to be cruel.

"What Lady Almeria means to say is that she and I were speaking of Miss Tennant, and I had stated that she had been often seen in your company these last few days."

This brought no flicker of understanding to Lord Coppinger's eyes, however.

"Is that so?"

Miss Madeley laughed, her eyes twinkling.

"You mean to say that you do not recall taking a walk with the particular young lady?"

Almeria watched the interaction as Lord Coppinger chuckled and shook his head and stated that no, he had not taken a walk specifically with a Miss Tennant, and did not know where the story had come from. Miss Madeley returned with a quip of her own, which made Lord Coppinger laugh and again, the vision of them standing up in church together had Almeria's mind burning.

She shook her head, trying to clear it from her thoughts.

"Are you quite alright, Almeria?" Lord Coppinger's hand touched hers and she started lightly, seeing his grey eyes searching hers, his fingers curling around her own in obvious concern. "You were shaking your head."

"Was I?" Thinking quickly, she looked away for fear that he would see the lie in her eyes. "I was only thinking about 'The London Ledger'. I do not know if you have seen what I placed within it, but I asked Lady Yardley to

THE EARL'S UNSPOKEN LOVE | 67

mention the flowers I have been receiving, in the hope that a gentleman would declare himself."

For some reason, Lord Coppinger went rather alarmingly pink in the face. His hand froze to hers, his eyes became a little wide, and his throat bobbed as he swallowed.

"I take it you did not know of this."

Miss Madeley looked from Lord Coppinger to Almeria and then back again, her eyes widening a little as though she understood something Almeria did not.

"No, I did not know. I have not looked at 'The London Ledger' as yet." Lord Coppinger cleared his throat. "I assume that no gentleman has yet claimed responsibility?"

She shook her head.

"No, they have not."

Embarrassed, and assuming that his surprise came from the fact that he had suggested she not do such a thing, she looked away. Was he frustrated that she had chosen to write in the Ledger, regardless?

"It was a little frustrating not to know." Miss Madeley seemed to feel the need to explain. "Given that another gentleman has shown some interest in Almeria, it is only right that she gives this fellow an opportunity to be upfront about his considerations of her. If it is the *same* gentleman, then all is well, is it not? But if it is someone entirely different, then..."

She shrugged and then looked away, her cheeks pinking, perhaps realizing that she had given away more than Almeria had wanted.

Lord Coppinger's now dark gaze swung slowly back towards Almeria, his jaw tightening a little.

"I assume that you are speaking of Lord Penforth." There was no explanation as to why she could not lift her gaze to his but, try as she might, her eyes seemed determined to look nowhere other than over his shoulder and thus, she merely nodded. "Well, I shall not be interrupted by him again." Lord Coppinger lifted his chin, seeming angry now. "Almeria, I must speak with you. Privately, in fact." Glancing around the room, he scowled. "Though it is not particularly easy to find a private space here in the ballroom, somewhere a little away from listening ears while remaining within sight of your mother."

"You need not tell me I ought not to have written in 'The London Ledger' or give me some warning about Lord Penforth." Almeria's lips twisted as he shot her a sharp look. She did not much like speaking to him this way, but his concern was much too great. "I am well able to take care of my own affairs in that regard. I understand that you are concerned for me, and I am certain that all you wish for is my happiness, in much the same way as I think of that for you also. Yet regardless, I am able to conduct affairs of the heart quite without your contribution – though I thank you for it."

Instantly, Lord Coppinger stepped closer and clasped her other hand with his. Almeria's breath tied itself in her chest as she gazed up into his stormy grey eyes. There was something different about him here, in this moment. Something which sent her heart into a flutter.

"It is not advice I wish to give you, Almeria. It is–"

"I have been found out!"

With a loud exclamation, Lord Penforth swept forward, practically knocking Lord Coppinger back as he swooped into a low bow before grasping her hand – which Lord Coppinger had only just dropped.

"Your determination has found me, then. I would have kept my secret a little longer, but alas, your note in 'The London Ledger' has forced me to reveal all."

Almeria froze in position, the air sticking in her throat as she looked directly back into Lord Penforth's face. His eyes were open wide, a broad smile across his face as he beamed back at her, clearly waiting for what he expected would be a delighted response.

Even though she had suspected her bouquets might very well be from Lord Penforth, the knowledge did not bring her any joy. Her heart did not leap with great exultation, her face did not set itself with smiles, nor could she find anything to say, for fear her seeming disappointment would echo itself through her words. Instead, she simply stood quietly as Lord Penforth gave a somewhat raucous laugh and clapped his hands together, as though overwhelmingly relieved that he could now tell her the truth.

"You mean to say that *you* sent all the bouquets?"

Miss Madeley sent a quick look to Almeria before turning her gaze to Lord Coppinger as Lord Penforth acknowledged that yes, this was so. Almeria cast a glance towards Lord Coppinger, then looked away, only to drag her gaze directly back to her friend. For whatever reason, Lord Coppinger was breathing heavily. His hands were balled into fists at his sides, his eyes flashing, his chin lifted and a scarlet red flush slowly covering his face. She could not understand it. Surely his dislike of Lord Penforth was not all that great?

"Lord Penforth, you are declaring yourself responsible for the bouquets Lady Almeria has been sent?"

Lord Coppinger appeared to be truly furious. His jaw was clenched, his eyes narrowed as he stuck his hands to his sides, practically demanding that Lord Penforth answer.

When Lord Penforth eagerly exclaimed that yes, it was he who was responsible, Lord Coppinger let out a furious exclamation and swung to one side, as though that was the only way he could damp down his emotions.

Almeria did not know what to say. There was no joy in the news that Lord Penforth was the one responsible for her flowers, and the way that Lord Coppinger was behaving was somewhat embarrassing. But before she could find something to say, Lord Coppinger had swung back towards Lord Penforth.

"How are you to prove that this is the truth? How will she know that you truly are the one responsible?" Almeria closed her eyes. In two days, no other gentleman had come to speak to her as yet. There was no need for Lord Coppinger to be so particular. "Well?" Lord Coppinger demanded, pushing out one finger towards Lord Penforth. "Perhaps you might tell her how many different flowers there were in her last bouquet, and what they were?"

Seeing Lord Penforth's eyebrows lift in obvious surprise at Lord Coppinger's question made Almeria all the more embarrassed.

"It would be easy enough to recall, knowing in my heart that roses are the flowers Lady Almeria desires the most."

Lord Penforth grinned, sending a knowing smile in Almeria's direction, but she only flushed, looking away. She must have mentioned to Lord Penforth at some point that her favorite flowers were roses, although she could not recall doing so.

Her brow furrowed, only for her to realize that every young lady in London would want to receive roses because of what they symbolized. That was what Lord Penforth meant.

But do I want Lord Penforth's admiration and affection?

The question was not one she was easily able to answer for, looking first at Lord Penforth and then to Lord

Coppinger, Almeria found her emotions blowing around wildly. It was as though she could not make sense of the moment, as if she could not say exactly what it was she felt in this situation. If Lord Coppinger was absent, would she feel any better? Or was it mere surprise over Lord Penforth's admission to her?

"We must dance," Lord Penforth swept into a bow. "I do hope that you have some dances remaining, Lady Almeria?"

Before she could answer, Lord Coppinger let out a snort of derision.

"One would have thought you might have made every effort to come to speak with Lady Almeria a good deal more quickly than this if you are so eager for her company." He rolled his eyes. "Do you not know how much her presence is sought after by the gentlemen of London?" His lip curled. "Neither have you answered my question as to how many there were of each of the two particular types of flower you sent in the last bouquet."

Sighing heavily, Almeria passed one hand over her eyes.

"Lord Coppinger, you need not defend me. I am quite able to make such judgments for myself." Seeing his narrowed eyes suddenly flare, she shrugged one shoulder lightly, then looked at Lord Penforth. "No, Lord Penforth, I have no dances remaining at present. Pray do forgive me."

And so saying, she took Miss Madeley's arm and stepped away from both gentlemen. The latter she had said had been a lie, of course, for she certainly *did* have some dances left on her dance card, she just did not wish to dance with Lord Penforth – and neither did she want to linger in his company when Lord Coppinger was there also. Seeing him standing there with that dreadful fury on his face had confused and embarrassed her, to the point that all she could think of doing was escape.

"Are you quite all right?" Miss Madeley looked at her, concerned. "You stepped away from them rather quickly, and I was sure that you had some dances remaining. Did you not want to step out with Lord Penforth? Not even after he has declared himself to be the gentleman who sent you the flowers?"

Shaking her head, Almeria let out a slow breath, aware of how it trembled.

"I am utterly overwhelmed," she answered truthfully, as Miss Madeley murmured sympathetically. "I know that I should be pleased. I thought I would be delighted to know who it was, but instead, I feel a strange sense of almost disappointment."

Miss Madeley twisted her lips for a moment, her brow a little lined as she thought.

"Are you disappointed because you have discovered who it is, or because it is Lord Penforth?"

The question stole Almeria's breath for a moment, her confusion growing all the more.

"I do not know." Her voice was weak, still shaking a little. "I do not know *what* emotion drives me at present. All I know is that I want to be free from both gentlemen."

Miss Madeley nodded.

"Then allow me to take you for another turn about the room, in the hope that we might find some more of our friends or even Lady Yardley. Although... might I ask you something?"

Almeria nodded.

"Of course."

"Did you note that Lord Coppinger stated that you had *two* types of flowers in your last bouquet?"

Having very little understanding as to the meaning of her friend's remark, Almeria shrugged.

"I must have said something to him about them. His behavior has been so very embarrassing, I am glad to be free of him also at present."

She said nothing more, but her thoughts continued to tumble around her mind, refusing to settle, refusing to land anywhere until her head began to ache. For the first time in her life, Almeria was glad of the pain in her head, hastily finding her mother and requesting that they return home. Her mother's concern for her daughter was immediate and thus Almeria soon found herself bundled in the carriage, with the horses heading towards home.

She could not have been more grateful.

CHAPTER EIGHT

"*T*he blasted fellow!" Lord Trevelyan watched with a look of mild amusement on his face as Marcus stalked around his drawing room. "This is not something to be laughed about either!" Throwing a furious look at his friend, Marcus threw up his hands. "You are meant to be showing sympathy, at the very least!"

"Then allow me to explain the reason for my smile." Rising from his chair, Lord Trevelyan poured two brandies from the drinks table, and then brought them back, handing one to Marcus and looking him straight in the eye. "Thus far, you have marched around my drawing room without giving a clear explanation for why you are doing so. I have heard something about Lady Almeria, and there is a wretched fellow involved also, but given that you have not told me his name nor explained what it is that he has done, I confess that I am quite at a loss."

It was this explanation which stole Marcus' ire away. Groaning, he rubbed one hand over his eyes.

"Forgive me, old friend. I thought that I had explained everything to you on at least three occasions already."

With a deep sigh, Lord Trevelyan sat back in his chair, spread out one hand, and lifted an eyebrow in question.

"I am ready to listen to you, Coppinger. However, might you begin at the very start, and tell me what has happened?"

Marcus swallowed against the swell in his throat, pushing his anger away.

"As you may know, Lady Almeria asked Lady Yardley to write an article in 'The London Ledger' on her behalf. It begged whichever gentleman had been sending her flowers to announce himself to her, for while she was delighted with him, it was a matter of frustration and intrigue that no name had been given. I discovered this in conversation with the lady at the ball last evening and was, I confess, on the verge of doing as she had asked. But before I could utter my words of truth, Lord Penforth threw himself forward with nothing but lies."

At this, the slight amusement which had lingered in Lord Trevelyan's eyes vanished. Instead, he sat forward in his chair, one hand at his chin, his eyes a little shadowed.

"You mean to say that Lord Penforth is the one who has claimed to be sending Lady Almeria the bouquets which you have been sending?"

Marcus nodded, the pain of it striking hard at his heart all over again.

"I do not know what to do." With a slight shrug, he took a sip of his brandy, lifting one shoulder. "Perhaps I should have told her the truth, regardless, but given how poorly I spoke to Lord Penforth thereafter, I was quite certain that I would then appear only to be attempting to discredit him."

Lord Trevelyan frowned.

"You say that you behaved poorly?"

Sighing, Marcus nodded.

"It is not something which I enjoy admitting to, but I was so angry, I made it quite clear that I did not believe him. I wanted him to prove, right then and there, that he was telling the truth, and thus demanded that he answer a question about the most recent bouquet... but Lady Almeria would not have it." Recalling her flashing eyes and the clear embarrassment in her warm cheeks, he winced. "She stated that no other gentleman had come forward as yet and, given that she had been waiting for some two days, therefore she did not require my aid in this matter."

"And had you thought to tell her yourself?"

"Except now that Lord Penforth has spoken first, I believe that Lady Almeria is convinced that he is the one who has sent her those flowers."

Lord Trevelyan scowled.

"Then you must continue to send them." Speaking quickly, Lord Trevelyan rose from his chair. "You must continue to send her flowers, as you have done before, without any note or any explanation as to whom they are from."

Not understanding this, Marcus frowned and watched his friend drop back into his chair.

"What would be the purpose of that?"

His friend spread out both hands, his brandy slopping from one side of his glass to the other.

"Because then she will wonder where they are coming from, if not from Lord Penforth."

Marcus' shoulders slumped.

"But would he not continue to do the same?" he suggested. "Might not Lord Penforth continue to tell her that *he* is the one sending these flowers, doing so simply to continue in the same fashion as he had done to deepen their connection?"

"He might do," Lord Trevelyan agreed. "Or his excuses and his explanations might wear thin, and Lady Almeria might find herself doubting his truthfulness. Would that not be a satisfactory outcome?"

Considering this for a few moments, Marcus pinched the bridge of his nose and let out a heavy sigh.

"But it is a path also fraught with difficulties. She might very well end up believing Lord Penforth, regardless."

Lord Trevelyan shook his head.

"Try as I might, I cannot believe that." He tilted his head. "You know Lady Almeria very well indeed. Why not use what you know of her to your advantage?" He sat a little further forward in his chair and pinned Marcus with a look. "From my perspective, you have two choices. Either you tell Lady Almeria the truth – that you are the one who sent her the bouquets, and that Lord Penforth is lying – and she will thereafter decide for herself how she is to respond. Or you do not... and risk Lord Penforth capturing her heart."

"But by telling her I might ruin our friendship entirely. She might be angry with me for never previously telling her the truth, for continuing with our simple friendship, when I felt something more."

Lord Trevelyan shrugged.

"An unfortunate consequence, perhaps, but yes. On the other hand, if you remain entirely silent and hope that she finds out the truth about Lord Penforth herself – or with aid from you, albeit without her knowledge, there is a great risk.... if she does discover that truth herself, then you have your opportunity, but if she does not...."

The weight of his unfinished sentence landed squarely on Marcus' shoulders. He nodded, rubbing one hand over his eyes.

"This is all my own doing," he muttered, growing angry

with himself for his lack of haste. "I have lacked the courage required to be honest with her about my feelings, and now look where I am. I am worse off than I was before. At least, before this, I still had hope."

"You still do," his friend responded quickly. "But you must act with all speed."

Marcus shook his head.

"Lady Almeria wants to marry for love." Grimacing, he looked away. "Of course, I would be willing to confess how ardently I love her, but I believe that she wants to love the gentleman in return. If she falls in love with Lord Penforth, then I must accept it. After all, she and I have known each other for long enough for her to have examined her heart. If there are no feelings at present, then perhaps, there will never be." He and Lord Trevelyan fell into silence and Marcus' shoulders slumped. There was no easy answer, no promise of a secure outcome, no matter what he did or said. With another long breath, he sat back in his chair and swirled his brandy around the glass. "Do you know what is truly terrible in all of this? What is the heaviest burden to bear?" he asked, staring at his brandy rather than at his friend. "It is the acknowledgment that this is all my own fault."

"Penforth."

Whether or not it was a good idea to speak to Lord Penforth directly, Marcus could not say for certain. However, his anger had pushed him to act, and regardless, he had every intention of speaking directly to Lord Penforth about what he had done.

"Good evening, old chap."

Lord Penforth smiled brightly, his expression rather jovial, but Marcus could think of nothing other than planting him a facer.

"I must speak with you." Marcus took a breath, steadying himself. "It is about Lady Almeria."

Instantly, Lord Penforth's eyebrow lifted.

"Lady Almeria," he repeated, as Marcus nodded. "You wish to talk to me about my acquaintance with her, no doubt feeling it is your brotherly duty."

Marcus blinked, suddenly confused.

"I am not her brother."

"Oh, I am well aware of that, but you are very close, are you not? It is almost as though you were her brother, which must indeed be your reason for wishing to speak to me about her. Are you concerned that I have some dishonorable intention?" Chuckling lightly, he waved a hand in an airy manner. "I can assure you; I am not that sort of gentleman."

Everything Marcus wanted to say suddenly disappeared. He had been about to state that *he* was the one in love with Lady Almeria and had been the one sending the bouquets. Now, however, he felt himself a little lost. If Lord Penforth saw him almost only as Lady Almeria's sibling, perhaps he ought to use that to his advantage, to make it quite clear that he would not stand for any ill treatment of the lady... which included any mistruths. Drawing himself up, he lifted his chin.

"You are quite right to suggest that I have some concern, Lord Penforth."

The gentleman spread his hands, a look of innocence passing across his features, his eyes a little wide, his expression open.

"But why should you say so? I have done no wrong as regards Lady Almeria."

The anger which threaded itself through Marcus' veins suddenly burned with a furious fire and it was all he could do not to exclaim furiously that the man had told nothing but a lie, had behaved falsely, and was not worthy of Lady Almeria's attentions. Taking a slow deep breath, he let it out again just as slowly, and then tilted his chin, looking Lord Penforth straight in the eye. Saying nothing, he let the moment settle into swirling tension, fully expecting Lord Penforth to buckle under the pressure and admit that he had, in fact, done something wrong as regarded the lady.

The longer he waited, however, the more apparent it became that the gentleman was not about to do anything of the sort. Lord Penforth's face became almost insolent, his eyes narrowing, but a small, dark smile pulling at his mouth as he practically dared Marcus to say precisely what it was that he had done.

I cannot hold myself back any longer.

"I know for certain that it was not you who sent the bouquets." The words demanded they be released. "You have built your acquaintance with Lady Almeria on nothing other than a lie."

The gentleman lifted one shoulder.

"Yes, I have." Much to Marcus' horror, Lord Penforth appeared entirely unfazed by the fact that Marcus had found him out. He shrugged and then yawned most rudely and conspicuously, as though to say that what Marcus had stated was entirely dull. "No other gentleman has come forward."

"It is not as though you gave them any reasonable time to do so!" Marcus threw up his hands. "The gentleman in question was considering what he ought to do. He is a quiet sort but has a great deal of affection for Lady Almeria. He deserved a chance to-"

Lord Penforth laughed and put one hand on Marcus' shoulder.

"My dear fellow, you are talking about me, it seems!" He laughed again, but Marcus' skin pinched with cold. "I have a great affection for Lady Almeria. I am also a gentleman, quite reserved, as I am sure it has been said of me, many a time, in society. If those are the only two things which you consider as regards to the gentleman who comes to court Lady Almeria, then might I suggest that you consider me in much the same favorable light as you consider this other fellow?" He tipped his head, grinning. "Mayhap you might offer me his name so that I can recognize my rival."

Marcus tightened his jaw but kept his expression clear of the anger which was burning through him.

"I have no intention of revealing this other fellow to you," he stated unequivocally. "Given that he sees me in much the same light as you have done - as more of a brother to Lady Almeria - he approached me with great care, speaking of his feelings and expressing himself to me most cautiously." This was, of course, a complete fabrication, but Marcus was not about to reveal to Lord Penforth that he, *himself,* had been the one sending flowers to Lady Almeria. "Given that I thought him most suitable, I therefore encouraged him to act in the way he thought best. He was about to tell Lady Almeria of his heart - I believe he was to do so on two occasions in fact, but was unfairly and unduly interrupted on both. And you then stole the final truth from his lips by telling Lady Almeria a lie. You are not the one who sent her those bouquets and I expect you to make that quite clear to her."

Lord Penforth considered this for a few moments, looking back at Marcus, who held his gaze so fixedly that his eyes began to water. After a few moments, however, Lord Penforth sighed and shook his head.

"And if I do not?"

Marcus threw him a dark look.

"If you do not, Penforth, then I shall tell Lady Almeria myself."

A slow smile spread across Lord Penforth's face, stealing away some of Marcus' confidence.

"But how shall you prove it? Will this supposedly shy, retiring fellow be willing to simply stand forward and tell Lady Almeria the truth? Will he and I have an argument in front of her, declaring that we are both as equally involved with these bouquets as the other? However is she to decide?"

Marcus clenched his hands into fists, barely controlling his fury. Lord Penforth was nothing but arrogance itself; selfish, inconsiderate, and entirely unwilling to look at anyone but himself. He did not care for Almeria, not in the way that she deserved. Marcus was sure of it.

"I shall tell you how." Taking a step forward, his jaw clenched, teeth gritting, he practically spat the words at Lord Penforth. "I know where he got his bouquets from. With you and with this other gentleman, I shall go there directly – with Lady Almeria also. I shall ask the shop-keeper directly which of the two gentlemen came into the shop and sent those flowers, along with the specific request to keep his name from her. What shall you do then Lord Penforth?" Much to Marcus's delight, Lord Penforth's face fell. His smile was gone in a moment, his eyes slowly darkening. There was no contentedness, no self-assurance in his face any longer. Instead, he looked distinctly frustrated. "You will tell her, Penforth." Marcus continued, "And you shall do so within the next few days, or I shall do it for you."

Quite certain that the victory was now his, Marcus turned away directly, keeping his head held high. There was nothing further he need do. Now Lady Almeria would learn that Lord Penforth was not the gentleman he purported to be. He was not truthful, he was not honest, and he was *not* a gentleman worthy of her – and Marcus would prove it to her, one way or the other.

CHAPTER NINE

"*I* am becoming increasingly drawn to you, Lady Almeria."

This was the most extraordinary thing for Lord Penforth to say. Thus far, Almeria had considered him a rather quiet sort, but for him to be so open now, so blunt about his feelings, was not something for which she was prepared.

"Thank you."

Blushing furiously, she turned her head away. The heat in her cheeks did not come from the fact that he offered her such feelings, but more because she did not know how to respond.

"I am so very grateful that you think well enough of me to accept my invitation for a walk."

"But of course."

Almeria kept her head turned away. She had accepted Lord Penforth's invitation for a walk, certainly, but Lady Yardley's words came back to her mind with force.

Just because a gentleman declares that he is in love with

you does not mean that you must therefore give him your heart to him in return. There is no obligation there.

Almeria had expected her feelings to change when Lord Penforth's confession had been made, but they had not. She was still disappointed that it was he who had made such a declaration, rather displeased that *he* had been the one to offer her flowers. Quite why she should feel such a way was somewhat perplexing, for she did, on the whole, enjoy his company. They usually had an excellent conversation, although she had to admit that he was still a little quiet on occasion. He was not often found in a large group of gentlemen and ladies, all conversing and laughing together - but then again, did she not appreciate that particular trait in Lord Coppinger also? He had always been a studious, thoughtful sort of person, and while she had teased him on occasion about such things, she had always appreciated his depth of thought. He usually gave great weight to what he said, which is why his outburst with Lord Penforth recently had been so surprising. It was highly unusual for him to display such a great fit of temper, and to exclaim so at Lord Penforth, simply because he did not believe that Penforth had sent her the bouquets of flowers – and this despite the fact that no one else had come to offer themselves to her either!

"I have lost you. I think."

Almeria looked to Lord Penforth, seeing his slightly indulgent smile and growing quickly embarrassed.

"Forgive me, I was lost in thought."

"And might I ask what you were thinking about?" Lord Penforth grinned, tilting his head as Almeria flushed all the more deeply. "It must have been something of great signifi-cance, I am sure, for it to take you away from our conversation like that when it is only you and I walking together. It must be very significant indeed."

"Perhaps it was." Almeria's reluctance to share her thoughts with him did not seem to be at all pleasing, for the smile on Lord Penforth's face immediately fell away. Almeria did not find herself at all encouraged to speak openly, however, and continued regardless. "I believe that you were telling me of your love of reading, were you not?"

She had only caught the slightest snippet of his conversation on the subject, but it seemed to bring him a little relief, for he smiled, nodded, and then began to speak further in the same vein. Almeria forced herself to pay attention, listening to him as he spoke of his love of literature, of how losing himself in the pages of some great book was a deeply satisfying pastime. She did enjoy reading, of course, but she certainly did not have the same passion for it as Lord Penforth displayed.

"And what is your favorite book?"

She glanced at him.

"I do not think that I have a particular favorite, for none have ever taken my attention in such a way." She smiled as Lord Penforth frowned. "Instead, I usually spend any time I have walking out of doors and, on occasion, I do enjoy painting."

"Or playing the pianoforte, no doubt."

Lord Penforth's smile was back, but she quickly shattered it with a shake of her head.

"Alas, I do not play the pianoforte. It is not my talent, as my music tutor soon discovered when he attempted to teach me the first scale over the course of six months - and I continually failed to grasp it."

Her lips curved as she recalled how Marcus had encouraged her to laugh over her lack of skill. He had been so helpful, for she had been very tearful indeed, afraid that she would not become a fine lady if she could not play an instrument. He had stated quite clearly that not all gentlemen required a young lady to be able to play the pianoforte, and they would still find her quite pleasing, regardless of what she did. When she had finally plucked up the courage to tell her father that she would much rather draw and paint than play the pianoforte, her father had instantly found her a tutor – and Marcus had continued his encouragements. Even in his latest letters, before they had met this Season, he had asked her whether or not she had continued with her painting.

"Again, I have lost you." Lord Penforth laughed, but there was a shadow in his usually pale blue eyes. "Are you troubled by something, Lady Almeria?"

"A little." Choosing to admit this to him, she offered him a quick look and a wry smile. "There are many things to consider when one is a young lady in society, I am afraid."

Lord Penforth's brows pulled together.

"Surely a young lady such as yourself has very little to concern herself with." His glib response made Almeria's mouth tug to one side. "After all, what is there for a young lady to do but to be admired as she goes about the place, finding herself pursued by various gentlemen until she sets her gaze upon one of them." He grinned. "Let us hope that I am one so fortunate, given that my affection is now turning into a deep love for you."

Almeria's dislike pushed a grimace across her expression. She did not much appreciate Lord Penforth's conversation, did not accept his promise of love, and even though she was fully aware that he was attempting to compliment her, she recoiled. Did he think her stupid? Lacking in good sense, or having no other interests outside having a gentleman admirer, and seeking a contented marriage?

Her chin lifted.

"You are quite mistaken, Lord Penforth." Hearing the tartness in her voice, she continued on firmly, making no effort to remove it from her tone. "There are a good many things on my mind at present, and certainly they do *not* simply revolve around various gentlemen."

Much to her frustration, Lord Penforth simply chuckled.

"I am very glad to hear it, for I should like your thoughts only to center upon myself, Lady Almeria."

Given that this was not at *all* what she had meant, Almeria bit her lip and looked away from him to prevent a sharp response from escaping. No doubt Lord Penforth thought that he was being clever by teasing her so, but she was not at all pleased.

"My thoughts do not center on any one gentleman whatsoever," she told him furiously, wanting to remove the rather smug look from his face. This, of course, was a lie, but Almeria was not about to inform him that she *was* thinking of a gentleman – albeit another gentleman entirely. "I was thinking on another matter, in fact."

"And will you share it with me?"

Almeria hesitated, her stomach twisting up inside herself over the lies she had now told. She had nothing to discuss with Lord Penforth, for she had not been thinking about anyone other than Lord Coppinger.

"No, not at present."

Lord Penforth chuckled again, and Almeria's stomach twisted harder.

"I see that I am not to be offered any of your secrets as yet." He sighed heavily, still smiling. "I will not take such a thing to heart, although mayhap I might share my thoughts with you." The smile on his lips fixed itself in place, seeming to Almeria almost false.

"Might I ask you if Lord Coppinger's behavior has concerned you of late? Is that who you have been thinking of, and why you have been so distracted?" Very surprised indeed to hear Lord Coppinger's name on Lord Penforth's lips, particularly after she had just stated that she was not thinking about any particular gentleman. Almeria merely lifted her eyebrows and waited. He grinned and shrugged both shoulders. "No doubt you will think me very rude indeed for asking, but it is only because I wonder whether or not you have been offered any particular information of late as regards his behavior."

Almeria blinked.

"His behavior?" she repeated, already confused. "Let me assure you, Lord Coppinger is the very best of gentlemen."

Lord Penforth did not immediately agree, however, tilting his head and looking at her, his steps slowing.

"Can you be quite certain of that?"

Coming to a standstill in the middle of the park, Almeria turned to face Lord Penforth directly.

I certainly am not enjoying his company and conversation any longer!

Taking a breath, she looked at him straight in the eye.

"I have known Lord Coppinger since we were children. We are *very* dear friends."

Lord Penforth sighed heavily and dropped his head.

"You will then be concerned to know that there have been some whispers about him."

Immediately, Almeria rolled her eyes, making her disdain obvious.

"Goodness, Lord Penforth! I did not think that you were the jealous sort! Why would you attempt to injure a fellow just because he has embarrassed you a little?"

Lord Penforth's smiles fled.

"Whatever do you mean?"

Quite certain that he knew *precisely* what he was doing at present, Almeria shook her head and sighed heavily.

"I am all too aware that Lord Coppinger spoke poorly when he saw you last. When you confessed about the bouquets, he was determined to prove that you were speaking the truth, rather than pretending to do so." She caught the flicker in Lord Penforth's gaze, caught his jaw flexing. "Of course, I understand why he did such a thing."

"And why was that?"

She smiled briefly.

"Because Lord Coppinger is like a brother to me," she told him firmly. "He is doing all that he can to aid me, to make certain that all is well, and that any gentleman who might wish to further their acquaintance with me is the very best of fellows. Lord Coppinger seeks only to protect me, that is all – but for you to attempt to discredit him simply because he has embarrassed you somewhat speaks poorly of you, Lord Penforth."

"And that is what you think I am trying to do, is it?"

Lord Penforth's eyebrows lifted, but Almeria did not change her opinion in the least.

"Yes, it is. I know Lord Coppinger almost as well as I know myself." Her eyes still held tight to his, unflinching. "I would not have anyone speak ill of him, and I would prefer you to not do so, Lord Penforth. If you have, in fact, heard something about him, it would be most unwise to simply believe it, would it not? That is the very *essence* of gossip, and not something I should give any consideration to, myself." She took a breath but spoke again before Lord Penforth could interject. "He and I are as close as siblings and, given that I could not think more highly of him, I would advise you to apply great caution before you even consider speaking ill of Lord Coppinger to me."

At this, Lord Penforth lifted his eyebrows but chose to say nothing.

Satisfied, Almeria turned, beginning to move down the path once more, with Lord Penforth falling into step beside her. She did not take his arm, however, and they walked forward in almost stony silence.

Some moments passed, but Almeria did not find herself at all willing to make conversation. Rather, she remained disgruntled with Lord Penforth. Quite certain that the only reason he had spoken so was simply to discredit Lord Coppinger in her eyes, she scowled and kept her gaze away from him. What sort of gentleman sought to return a slight in such a way as this?

"You are mistaken."

Almeria lifted an eyebrow, barely glancing at Lord Penforth.

"I beg your pardon?"

"You are mistaken," he repeated firmly. "I do not say anything about Lord Coppinger in an attempt to discredit him. I say it out of legitimate concern for you. As you say, you are as close as siblings, but might it not then be wise to be careful in your connection with him, if he is found to be a little lacking in some regard?"

Almeria resisted the urge to roll her eyes again, choosing instinctively not to believe him.

"As I have made quite clear, Lord Penforth, I have no intention of either listening to, or believing, anything that is said or whispered about Lord Coppinger, which includes from you."

"Wait." Lord Penforth stopped, turned, and catching her hand before she could snatch it back, looked deeply into her eyes. "Does that mean that you do not believe I have a genuine affection for you? You do not think that what I say is true, which must mean that you view me in a deeply unfavorable light."

Almeria opened her mouth, only to snap it closed again. Was she being unfair to Lord Penforth? Mayhap she ought to reconsider, for even though she did not believe anything said about Lord Coppinger, Lord Penforth might be speaking of something he was concerned about, rather than simply doing so for his own ends.

But that does not mean that I think well of him, particularly not at this juncture.

"I did not ever say such a thing." Speaking plainly, she held his gaze steadily. "But my considerations still stand." Pulling her hands away from his, she folded them across her chest so that he could not take her hand again. "I have seen the interplay between you. Therefore, is it understandable that I would consider where your supposed *concern* for Lord Coppinger might come from..."

"I can see that." There was a slight softness to his tone, something she had not heard before. "But I believe you underestimate me, Lady Almeria. I am not as foolish a gentleman as you might think me." This last part stung rather painfully, and Almeria turned away sharply. "We are not yet particularly well acquainted, as you might recall." Lord Penforth swung into step beside her again, a slight smile playing around the edges of his mouth. "Which I suppose is a satisfactory excuse."

A little irritated, and feeling as though she was being

chastised by an older sibling or even a parent, Almeria curled the edge of her lip.

"I am quite able to make my own judgments on matters such as this, Lord Penforth."

"Then I shall have to prove it to you. I suppose. As I have said, I overheard a whisper about Lord Coppinger's conduct. I shall not share such whispers with you unless you request it, of course, but I should ask you to be careful. In fact, I should almost insist upon it."

She shook her head.

"I do not need your advice, and nor do I want to hear anything about Lord Coppinger." How much she was beginning to dislike this gentleman, how much she disliked his insistence that she do as *he* thought best, particularly since their acquaintance had been of so short a duration. "Lord Coppinger and I shall be just as we have always been."

"And if I am proven correct?" Lord Penforth lifted an eyebrow. "If what I have warned you about proves to be legitimate, then might you not consider me, and my promised affection, to be entirely genuine?"

Considering this for a moment, Almeria nodded, holding his gaze boldly.

"Yes, Lord Penforth, I shall accept it and will hear whatever you have to say about him, but for the moment, please, do not tell me of any whispers as regards Lord Coppinger. Society is as it has always been, and it does, on occasion, seek to pull down those who are of a very worthy standing, simply so that they may be as lowly as the person making up such falsehoods." She offered a wry smile. "After all, there are a good many people who dislike a fellow simply because of how highly he stands in society, of how well he is seen by other members of the *ton*. I should not like any difficulty to come to Lord Coppinger by such a simplistic emotion as jealousy."

Wondering if her words were hitting hard against Lord Penforth's heart, she saw him scowl and felt her own heart lift with satisfaction.

Lord Penforth cleared his throat and dropped his gaze to the ground.

"I do hope that he knows how much he ought to treasure you as his champion." The words came with a slight edge to them as his smile faded. "Would that I should be so lucky as to have someone speak so highly of me, regardless of what has been said."

"I am certain that you do the very same for a sister or a brother of your own, Lord Penforth."

"Alas, but we shall never know," he replied in a much more jovial tone, as though everything they had just discussed had no great importance. "I have no siblings, it is only myself. Therefore, I take great care of my acquaintances and even more so those I consider... important."

This last part was, of course, directed towards her, but Almeria did not smile at him when he offered his arm. She hesitated, hating that she was obliged to take it, and clamping her mouth shut firmly. She did not want to walk with him, did not want to be in his company, not when he had upset her by talking about Lord Coppinger in such a manner. She was greatly irritated to hear the lack of consideration in his words – and suddenly, the very last person she wished to be in company with was very gentleman she was forced to spend the rest of the afternoon beside.

CHAPTER TEN

"*N*o, he has done nothing."

Marcus shook his head as he and Lord Trevelyan watched Lord Penforth. The man was doing nothing but enjoying himself, laughing at something which had been said to him by another. He did not even glance in Marcus' direction. And indeed, Marcus was quite certain that the gentleman had not even noticed his arrival in White's.

"What do you intend to do?" Lord Trevelyan shook his head in disgust, picked up his whisky, and finished it in one gulp. "The man is a disgrace."

"I am well aware of that." Marcus tilted his chin towards Lord Penforth. "He does not deserve Lady Almeria and therefore, my only intention at present is to make certain that she knows the truth. I have given him the opportunity to tell her, and he has not done so."

"You have asked her?"

Marcus nodded.

"We spoke this afternoon. Almeria was somewhat distressed over her time with Lord Penforth yesterday afternoon. She would not tell me anything particular, only that she had found herself rather upset by his company and conversation."

Marcus allowed himself a small smile as Lord Trevelyan chuckled.

"Then mayhap all will be well. It seems as though you have very little concern as to their prolonged acquaintance."

Hesitating, Marcus shook his head.

"I am not quite certain about that." His smile faded. "I have a suspicion that the gentleman is determined to get whatever he desires by any means necessary. After all, he has already lied to Almeria about the flowers, simply because he desired to be her champion and the one she would consider. Even when he was being told of the truth, he simply laughed at the fact that another fellow had been intending to confess all to the lady. He did not care. There was very little indication that he had even a small hint of conscience over the matter. No, Trevelyan, Lord Penforth is not a gentleman to be ignored. He will not give up the lady easily, regardless of whether or not *she* desires him."

"But if Lady Almeria herself has no desire to be courted by him, then you need not be at all worried."

"Unless..." Grave concern rose in Marcus' heart. "Unless it is that Lord Penforth would go as far as to force the lady's hand." He shook his head. "I have always considered him to be a quiet fellow, but after our incident, I see that he is cunning along with being quiet." A bark of laughter from Lord Penforth came to them across the room, and Marcus rolled his eyes. "Though on this occasion, he is rather raucous."

"Perhaps a product of a little too much liquor."

Lord Trevelyan snorted as Marcus nodded.

"I am concerned that he is much more calculating than I

ever believed and that, in return, worries me about how he would treat Almeria."

"All the more reason for you to tell her the truth."

Marcus' lips twisted, for he knew that his friend was correct. There was no need for him to wait any longer. He had done the gentlemanly thing of allowing Lord Penforth the opportunity to tell Almeria the truth - but since he had not done so, Marcus had no other choice but to speak to the lady herself.

"It does make me wonder about why he has chosen Lady Almeria."

"Might I ask you something?" Lord Trevelyan tilted his head. "You *are* aware that Lady Almeria is the daughter of a Marquess, are you not?"

A little surprised at this, Marcus lifted an eyebrow.

"Of course I am."

"Then you should not wonder about why Lord Penforth might seek to attach himself to the lady. Yes, he is an Earl but not all Earls are wealthy. What an advantage it would be for him within society, to be wed to the daughter of a Marquess! I am certain that his coffers would increase also."

A ball of panic began to roll around Marcus' stomach as he caught the edge of his lip between his teeth.

"I understand what you mean." It was unfortunate, but many a young lady was considered only for her merits with respect to her father's title and the wealth which she might bring to the gentleman she was to marry, as well as whether or not she was of good breeding. Marcus silently prayed that Lord Penforth was not looking at Almeria in such a way, for even that would only add to the darkness of his character. How much there was of Lady Almeria to be admired. How highly he himself thought of her! "I have never told her."

"What was that?"

Marcus shook his head and passed a hand across his eyes, unwilling to tell Lord Trevelyan exactly what he had been thinking. With a small sigh, he shrugged his shoulders.

"I should have done more when it came to Almeria. I should have spoken to her sooner and with a good deal more urgency. Had I done so, then perhaps she – and we also – might never have been in this circumstance."

His friend grimaced.

"That may be so, but you cannot blame yourself. It is not as though you were aware that Lord Penforth would behave in this manner. He has not exactly proven himself to be an excellent fellow, has he? You had every intention of speaking honestly to Lady Almeria, planning what you would say to her once your bouquets had been sent." His scowl grew as he turned his gaze across the room. "It is Lord Penforth who is at fault here, not you."

His friend's words brought him a little relief and, accepting this with a grunt, Marcus glanced in the same direction as Lord Trevelyan, only to sit up straight as he saw the gentleman rise.

"Look he is leaving. I must speak to him now before he has any opportunity to slip away."

"I shall come with you."

Together, the two men rose from their chairs, following Lord Penforth as he left White's. It was unfortunate, however, that many other gentlemen began to come into the establishment at the same time as they were trying to leave, pushing them back into the place, and by the time they had stepped outside, it was very difficult indeed to see where Lord Penforth had gone.

"Hey, hold up now!"

The voice came to them over the crowd, and Marcus' arm was quickly grabbed by Lord Trevelyan.

"Look. There he is – that was he calling to a hackney."

"A hackney?" In the dim moonlight, Marcus hurried forward. "We should catch him. I *must* speak with him."

"It is very odd," Lord Trevelyan puffed, just as Lord Penforth climbed into the hackney, shouting instructions that Marcus could not hear. "Why does he not go to his carriage?"

Something fierce grasped hold of Marcus' heart and he practically ran towards his own carriage, waving one hand.

"Do come on, Trevelyan!"

"Yes, my Lord?"

The coachman made to come down from his seat, but Marcus gestured for him to remain.

"No, no. Quickly, follow that hackney!"

Within seconds, the door was closed with Marcus and Lord Trevelyan inside – and the carriage hastily pulled away. Marcus leaned forward in his seat, as though it would somehow push the carriage a little faster, and urge it a little more quickly towards the hackney which was carrying Lord Penforth.

Lord Trevelyan cleared his throat.

"I thought you were going to *speak* to the fellow, Coppinger. Now it seems that we are following him."

Aware that he had acted impulsively, Marcus kept his gaze turned away, even though he could see very little in the darkness.

"My desire to speak to him is very urgent indeed and, given that we know he has a disagreeable character already, would it not be wise to find out where he is going this late in the evening? Lady Almeria ought to know."

"I suppose that may be so, but all the same..." Lord Trevelyan replied, but Marcus merely shrugged and continued speaking.

"It is very strange, is it not? Why would Lord Penforth leave his carriage behind and go in a hackney? I arrived at White's only a few minutes after him and saw his carriage waiting outside White's. I am certain that it will still be there – and besides which, we are not moving in the direction of his townhouse."

Lord Trevelyan grimaced.

"We are not, you are quite right. I suppose it is all very unusual," he admitted quietly. "I confess that I also find myself with an eagerness to know precisely what he is doing now."

Managing a smile, Marcus kept his eyes fixed on the window, looking out into the gloom. He could not fully explain his sudden desire to follow Lord Penforth. Perhaps it was the fact that he wanted to throw in Penforth's face the fact that Lady Almeria would know all by the time tomorrow came. Perhaps it was because he wished to know precisely what Lord Penforth was doing. Regardless, there was something about the fellow that he did not like, and thus he found the drive to follow him more than overwhelming. It was not something he could resist, and thus he chased after Lord Penforth, determined to have spoken to him by the time the evening was out.

"All the same, this is rather ridiculous." Lord Trevelyan muttered into the darkness. "We are following Lord Penforth with very little idea of where he is going. What if he is simply going to visit a relative?"

"At this hour?" In the silence which followed, Marcus let out a slow breath. "Regardless of where he is going, I *must* speak with him. The fact that he has stolen the opportunity for me to confess my love to Almeria means that I must tell him outright that he will be unmasked. I will not allow him to have any sort of victory when it comes to Almeria."

Lord Trevelyan sighed.

"I should not like to be in love, I do not think. To my mind, it makes one behave in a most unusual manner. "

Marcus allowed his friend's remarks to fall into silence, looking out still at the London streets and seeing very little which he recognized. It was late and, therefore, very dark, and there were only a few lamps lit. However, all the same, he still realized very quickly that they were no longer anywhere near the area of London which he knew well. In fact, they were now driving through a part of London that he would usually wish to avoid.

"Trevelyan," he murmured, as his friend grunted in reply. "I believe that we are now within the East End of London."

There came a few moments of silence before Lord Trevelyan shuffled across in his seat, coming to look out of the window opposite the one which Marcus stared out of.

"Are you certain?"

"Yes." Marcus' stomach tensed, his sense of foreboding rising. "Perhaps I can now understand why Lord Penforth did not take his carriage."

Lord Trevelyan cleared his throat.

"At this point, my own curiosity is piqued – although yes, mayhap we ought to have hailed a hackney also." He took in a deep breath, then looked towards Marcus. The dim light from a lantern flickered briefly across his face for just a moment, revealing a heavy frown. "Whatever is Lord Penforth doing here?"

Marcus shook his head, grimacing.

"I must find out, Trevelyan. I must discover what he is here for, even if he still manages to convince Lady Almeria that he sent those bouquets simply because he was so desperate for her affection. I will need something else by which to convince her to stay away from him."

"I understand."

There was no question in Lord Trevelyan's voice. He sounded very serious indeed, not even a flicker of mirth in his usually cheerful voice. The silence continued and both men sat quietly, waiting for the hackney they were following to come to a stop. The carriage wheels rattled across the cobbled streets until, finally, they halted.

"We must go. Lord Penforth has stepped out." In a moment, Marcus was out of the carriage, leaving Lord Trevelyan to follow him. He stepped onto the dark street, barely able to see more than a few feet in front of him. They were surrounded by buildings with only a few dim lights emanating from the windows. There was certainly something untoward here, something Marcus did not like. Recoiling towards the carriage, he looked towards his friend, who immediately scowled.

"The East End of London holds many shadows." Lord Trevelyan folded his arms heavily across his chest, as though somehow that would protect him from the encroaching blackness which seemed to be more than just the usual evening's darkness. "Did you see where Lord Penforth went?"

Marcus was not immediately able to answer, his eyes still becoming used to the darkness as he cast an eye over the street. Hearing the sound of a door slamming, he caught the barest flicker of movement, then pointed one finger to a building to their left.

"There. Perhaps it is a place where other gentlemen of note meet, far away from the confines of society."

"Then let us go, but be cautious."

Nodding, Marcus began to hurry in the direction of the door, putting one hand on the handle. A small lantern flickered just outside the building, revealing a red door. Squaring his shoulders, Marcus pushed his way carefully inside, hearing the noise of raucous laughter and conversation reaching out toward him. The moment he made his way into the room, however, the sound swiftly began to die away as every single person turned to look at both himself and Lord Trevelyan. Realizing immediately that they had become the object of everyone's attention, he cleared his throat. It seemed as though every other man present sitting within the establishment was not a gentleman, as he had suspected might be the case.

Whatever this establishment was, Marcus was utterly certain that they had just stepped into significant danger.

CHAPTER ELEVEN

"*Y*ou looking for Mr. Stepson?"

A man who had been sitting behind a long, wooden counter at the side of the room came slowly to his feet.

"Stepson?" Marcus repeated, before quickly nodding and smiling in an attempt to appear confident, even though he had very little understanding of the situation he had stepped into. "Yes. I need to speak with him."

"Well, you can't." The man grinned, coming from behind the counter and wandering closer to Marcus as the rest of the men in the room kept their gazes trained on him. "He's already got some men in there. You should have come another night. There won't be any more gambling deals done tonight."

Marcus swallowed and glanced at Lord Trevelyan, seeing his friend's eyebrow lift. Lord Penforth was here to gamble? He recalled Lord Trevelyan's concerns over Lady Almeria's wealth and the fact she was the daughter of a Marquess. Was that why Lord Penforth sought her?

Looking the man straight in the eye, he tilted his head.

"You speak of Lord Penforth?"

Lord. Trevelyan, who had come to stand beside him, boasted a confident air.

"We seek Lord Penforth. We are friends of his, you see. We followed him in case there should be any trouble."

The man's eyebrows lifted and he grinned broadly as a few murmurs ran around the room.

"Trouble?" he repeated, as a few of the men now laughed boldly alongside the broad-shouldered man, making Marcus' skin prickle. "Now why would you think there might be any trouble?"

Marcus cleared his throat, deeply uncomfortable.

"No, of course there wouldn't be any difficulty here. I mean, there is not any trouble of any sort usually, of course, but it is always wise to be careful."

He knew that he was blabbering, attempting to make sense of a situation where he had no understanding whatsoever, but what else was there for him to do?

Again, the man chuckled.

"Yes, I suppose that's true, but I've got no knowledge about whether or not you *are* really friends of this Lord Penforth. If you are friends, then he should have told you that we don't do names around here." His smile faded, a darkness flashing across his expression as he lowered his head just a little, glowering at them both. "Which I think means you'd both better be leaving."

At that very moment, a door to Marcus' left opened and, shortly after that, Lord Penforth stepped out. There was nowhere for Marcus and Lord Trevelyan to hide. Lord Penforth's eyebrows lifted, and he blinked in obvious surprise. Taking a second, Marcus lifted his chin, thinking silently to himself that he ought to take hold of the man's surprise and use it to his advantage.

I must appear confident.

"Penforth." Aware that he had only two choices – one being to admit that he had arrived here unexpectedly and did not know what to expect at the present moment, or the other to feign confidence and make it quite clear to Lord Penforth that he was in control of this moment. He chose the latter, intending to state quite clearly that Lord Penforth had failed to tell Lady Almeria the truth, and to make it quite clear that Lady Almeria would know of all Lord Penforth had done. He took a breath. "I knew you would not be suitable for Lady Almeria. Now I have the proof."

Lord Penforth made his way toward Marcus and Lord Trevelyan, his eyebrow lifting as everyone else in the establishment continued to watch them.

"And what business have you following me?"

"I have every business," Marcus announced firmly. "You know that I am closely acquainted with Lady Almeria. I now come to make certain that you are not about to do whatever you can to steal her away. She is the daughter of a Marquess, and no doubt has a great dowry - a substantial fortune which will come with her when she marries. *You* shall not have your hands upon any of it."

Much to Marcus' disconcertment, Lord Penforth chuckled.

"Yes, I shall." Coming closer to him, he tilted his head. "I do not think that there is anything you can to do prevent it either."

"You have a great deal of confidence for a man who has just been discovered in one of the gambling dens here in the East End." Lord Trevelyan snorted, clearly as irritated as Marcus. "What sort of young lady would willing attach themselves to a gentleman such as you?"

Lord Penforth tilted his head, now only a few steps away from Marcus.

"A young lady such as Lady Almeria, would 'willingly attach themselves', as you say it, so long as they did not know anything about this particular situation." He shrugged. "It is not as though you know the specifics of this situation and thus, she shall not either."

Marcus snorted derisively, ignoring the rattle of unease in his chest.

"And what makes you think that I will not tell Almeria of this? Regardless of whether or not I know precisely what has taken place, I know where we are and what this place is." Lord Penforth opened his mouth, but Marcus continued quickly. "You know very well that I am already to tell her that you did not send those bouquets. How glad I am to know that you will not be able to pretend anything more, that you won't be able to invent some excuses about why you are so very much in love with her that you simply had to do such a thing as lie about the flowers! She will know precisely the sort of gentleman you are, and I will be glad to see you separated."

"So that you might take my place." Lord Penforth tilted his head, his eyes glittering. "Do not think me a fool. I did not believe a word of your statement that some other gentleman gave those bouquets to Lady Almeria, for I am certain that it was you. *You* are the one who is in love with Lady Almeria, and the one who did not have the boldness to tell her so!" Chuckling, he grinned at Marcus, no trace of doubt in his eyes. "This is not about the fact that you think I am unsuitable for her, but rather that you regret your lack of courage."

Drawing himself up, Marcus lifted his chin, ignoring the heat building in his frame.

"I will not be drawn into any sort of discussion about my character, rather than looking at you and what you have done." His jaw tight, he looked away to Lord Trevelyan. "You have been discovered in lies, you have been found here and I have Lord Trevelyan with me. He can attest to what we have seen, even though, no doubt, you will do nothing but lie about what you were doing here. Thankfully," he finished, bolstered with confidence now, "Lady Almeria trusts me."

"It is not about my own circumstances that I might choose to lie." Instantly, Marcus' confidence began to falter. "I might choose to lie about both you *and* Lord Trevelyan, in fact."

Marcus frowned, about to say that there was none here except for the ruffians who sat around the tables, only for the door to his left to open again and, much to Marcus' horror, he saw three other gentlemen come out to stand in the room. Their eyes flicked to him, but none came forward, all standing stock still just outside the door.

"So you see that I am firmly in control." Lord Penforth laughed softly, coming even closer to Marcus and putting one hand on his shoulder as he looked him straight in the eyes. "There is your choice, Lord Coppinger. If you tell Lady Almeria what you have discovered of me, then the lies I shall tell about you *and* Lord Trevelyan will spread like a furious fire through society – with my words encouraged by the other gentlemen I have here." He lifted one shoulder. "*Or* you can stay silent, and allow my pursuit of Lady Almeria to continue without hindrance." After glancing over his shoulder, he looked back at Marcus with a lifted eyebrow. "Now, might I suggest that you depart and think upon your choice? These gentlemen are soon to join me, and I should think it unwise for you to linger."

Marcus was not a gentleman to be afraid, but looking around the room and seeing all of the other men sitting at tables, as well as the gentlemen standing to the side, watching the conversation with great interest, he felt himself falter. There was the chance that this might soon become an all-out brawl should he linger, for his own temper was already flaring. He was not about to let Lord Penforth win, however, and thus he stood exactly where he was. He was angry – angry that Lord Penforth thought he could do such a thing as this, could treat Almeria with such disdain – and when Lord Penforth laughed, his temper grew hot. It felt as if fire billowed within him, sending smoke into his veins as he lifted one hand and knocked Lord Penforth's hand from his shoulder with great force.

Lord Penforth's smile immediately shattered

"I have every belief that Lady Almeria will believe me, should I tell her everything," he stated, furiously, his voice low as Lord Trevelyan put a calming hand on his arm. "She and I are as close as we have ever been. She knows me. She trusts me, and she believes what I say. There is nothing she would hold against me. If I tell her that what I say is the truth, then you can be certain, Lord Penforth, that she will not doubt even a single word."

Marcus smiled grimly, believing that such a statement would foil Lord Penforth's grand plan. He was rather taken aback when the man simply shrugged.

"Be that as it may, would you really have her attach herself to a gentleman whose reputation will be quite ruined?" Lord Penforth tilted his head, his eyes gleaming. "For that is what you would be doing, Lord Coppinger – ensuring that your own reputation is entirely ruined. Even if you told her the truth, she would be all too aware that the *ton* believed something entirely different about you, given what I and my friends will say. Do you really think that her father – being a Marquess – would allow his daughter to wed a scoundrel such as yourself?"

The air seemed to grow thick as Marcus stared at Lord Penforth, feeling as though he had slipped over the edge of a precipice, and was now clinging to the top for dear life. Trying to push a little confidence into himself, he took in a deep breath and set his shoulders.

"There are many other ways for gentlemen and a lady to commit themselves to each other rather than simply seeking her father's approval."

"But I could not imagine you would allow such a scandal to touch the reputation of Lady Almeria."

Lord Penforth's grin had returned, and Marcus slowly felt his grip on the conversation slipping. It seemed that Lord Penforth was more devious than Marcus had ever imagined.

"Why?" Lord Trevelyan stepped forward, his hand on Marcus' shoulder, pulling him back a little, obviously seeing the way that Marcus had curled one hand into a fist. "Why are you doing this? What is it about Lady Almeria that you desire so greatly? Is it because of her title? Her father's fortune?"

"That is none of your business, Trevelyan." Lord Penforth scowled, then made a shooing motion with his hand. "Now be off with you for, as I have said, these men will not take kindly to you lingering."

Despite the anger burning through him, Marcus slowly began to realize – through a haze of red fire – that there was nothing else he could do other than step away. Feeling the encouragement of Lord Trevelyan's hand, he took a sharp breath, his jaw set – and lunged for Lord Penforth. To his dark delight, the man flinched and stepped back, recoiling sharply.

"You will not succeed."

With the confidence still burning through his words, Marcus turned and walked from the room, only for his shoulders to slump as he stepped out onto the street. His mind began to whirl with thoughts, but none gave him a clear path, a way forward. A groan escaped him.

"We will find a way out of Lord Penforth's trap," Lord Trevelyan promised softly. "You are right to say that Lady Almeria would believe you. I would tell her the truth anyway."

Marcus swallowed as the darkness surrounded them, feeling it weighing down upon him all the heavier.

"And yet, Lord Penforth is correct to state that I might injure her reputation should she ever decide to attach herself to me. Besides, I could not simply confess my love and then push myself away from her! It would not do her any good."

"But you cannot let her continue her acquaintance with Lord Penforth!" his friend exclaimed, sounding quite horrified as Marcus simply shook his head. "The lady has a right to know about the scandal."

"I am aware of that – and should Lord Penforth seek to court her, then I will tell her everything, regardless of what happens thereafter."

Peering out into the darkness, seeking the waiting carriage, Marcus searched his mind for an answer which would not only protect Lady Almeria but would also save his own reputation – but nothing offered him any light. It was as though everywhere he looked was covered in shadows – much like these dark streets – and thus, he was without even the smallest ray of light and without the smallest flicker of hope. Finding the carriage, he climbed into it, sat forward, put his elbows on his knees and dropped his head.

"We will find a way. Your reputation will not be injured."

Lord Trevelyan's encouragements settled in Marcus' mind, but did not bring him any relief. Lord Trevelyan could not offer him a solution, could not tell him what he ought to do, and thus, Marcus could not see a clear way forward. Unless he came up with his own idea, unless he could see a way to prevent all of Lord Penforth's threats from falling down upon him, he would have to do just as his enemy had demanded.

CHAPTER TWELVE

"*A*nd how are things progressing with Lord Penforth?"

Almeria hesitated.

"It is very difficult to say," she said, after a moment. "I confess that I find him a rather difficult gentleman at times, but on other occasions, he is very charming indeed."

It had been three weeks now, since Lord Penforth had confessed to her the truth about the flowers and, while he had not yet asked to court her, Almeria was certain that such a thing would soon occur. When that was put to her, however, she was not sure what she would say and, to her mind, it seemed as though he was somewhat aware of her reluctance. While Lord Penforth had mentioned the possibility of speaking to her father, he had not yet done so.

"If I may be so bold, you do not appear to be particularly enamored of the gentleman, I must say."

Almeria looked at Miss Madeley.

"That is because I am not," she informed her friend, who immediately nodded as though she understood entirely. "And besides that, there is something – nay, someone, who is a good deal more on my mind. I am certain that it is only his absence which has me so often considering him, but all the same, he is there nonetheless."

She was relieved that she could be honest with Miss Madeley, for her friend nodded and smiled softly, no judgment in her expression or her voice.

"You are speaking of Lord Coppinger, are you not?"

"I am." Almeria nodded, having no desire to hide such a thing. Lord Coppinger had been markedly absent from her company these last three weeks, and she had found that more distressing than she had ever imagined she might. "I have spoken to him of course, but he is not as friendly as he once was. It is as though the closeness we shared has somehow lessened, and I am very troubled by that."

"But is not such a thing quite natural?" Miss Madeley frowned, glancing up at Almeria as they walked in the sunshine through the park. "After all, he is seeking a bride and you are seeking a husband. You shall not have the same closeness as you once did. That should be expected, if not a little encouraged, perhaps."

Almeria nodded, but her friend's words did not settle her mind. Instead, she found herself all the more distressed. It was as if having this truth offered to her was a sword that pierced her heart.

"But that is not what I want."

The words came out before she was ready to have them spoken but, to her relief, Miss Madeley only smiled.

"Then what is it that you want?"

Almeria did not even have to consider her answer.

"I want us to be as close as we once were. I want us to be dear friends, able to share with each other whatever we say, think, and feel at the time. I do not like the fact that he does not spend as much time in my company as he once did.

I know that all that you have said is quite true and, no doubt, I am being very foolish in speaking as I am, but that is the truth of it. You ask what I want? *This* is what I want, for it is what I am missing at present, and what I find very difficult to bear." They walked in silence for some minutes, and although Almeria glanced towards her friend, Miss Madeley said nothing. Her eyes were fixed on the path ahead of them, and though she remained quiet, Almeria knew that her friend was simply considering things. Miss Madeley was always very thoughtful, and did not speak without carefully deliberating what it was that she wanted to say. "It is foolish, I know." Unable to bear the silence, Almeria spoke again, her heart twisting painfully as though admitting such a thing was agonizing in itself. "It is not as though he appears to have any difficulty in pushing himself away from me."

The ache in her heart redoubled and she was forced to suck in a breath. She looked for Lord Coppinger whenever they were out in society at a ball or a soiree. She could not recall the last time that they had danced together, and was a little surprised at how much she longed for such a thing now, how much she desired to be back in his arms. Why was he ignoring her? Was it, as Miss Madeley suggested, quite natural? Was this something she ought to simply accept? But if it was, why was she caused so much tumultuous pain by it?

"I think it is quite normal to feel sorrow when a relationship one has known for so long begins to take a different turn." Miss Madeley's voice was soft, seeming to understand all that Almeria felt. "But if you do not want such a thing to change, Almeria, you must question what it is you seek instead."

"I do not know what I seek, other than Lord

Coppinger's company." Almeria flung up her hand as Miss Madeley simply nodded, ready to listen to yet another outpouring of whatever was bubbling inside Almeria. "This change is not one I find at all pleasing. Yes, of course. I was aware such a thing would happen now that we are both looking for a husband or a wife, but it does not please me, I had thought..." Trailing off, she dropped her hand back to her side, surprised that tears were now forming in her eyes. "I had thought that we would always be close."

Miss Madeley smiled and tilted her head a little closer to Almeria.

"Well, if that is what you want, then that is what you must pursue."

Almeria shook her head, aware of the trembling in her voice.

"But how can such a thing be? You are quite right to say that we are now in a new situation in our lives, one where he seeks a bride and I seek a husband. It is normal and right for us to change, for our connection to become a little different. I am simply struggling with that particular idea. Mayhap all I require is a little time to become used to the difference. Yes, that is all, I am sure."

Even as she spoke, her foolish heart gave her another flare of pain, and she squeezed her eyes closed for a minute.

"*I* do not think you desire such a thing as that." Miss Madeley frowned as Almeria looked to her, startled. "Perhaps it is Almeria, that you care for Lord Coppinger."

Her heart slammed hard against her ribs and Almeria blinked.

"Care for him?" The idea was almost preposterous. "Good gracious, no!"

"You need not look as shocked as that." Laughing, her friend tilted her head, squinting at Almeria. "My very dear

THE EARL'S UNSPOKEN LOVE | 117

friend, could you not have noticed how much your heart has quickened whenever Lord Coppinger draws near? Could you truthfully say that you have never found yourself watching him with admiring eyes?

"I..."

To her utter embarrassment and complete shock, Almeria found that she could not answer the question. Miss Madeley laughed softly, but it was not a laugh of mockery.

"Almeria, I saw your reluctance when I first mentioned Lord Coppinger, and how handsome he was. It became clear to me that you were not particularly enamored of the idea of him becoming acquainted with a young lady such as myself, who might, one day, become his bride."

Flushing, Almeria immediately tried to explain, stuttering as she did so.

"No, indeed, it is not that I thought you an unsuitable match. It is only that –"

"Pray, be at peace." Pressing Almeria's arm, Miss Madeley silenced her protests. "I can understand that this may come as a great shock to you, and I certainly will not seek to embarrass you further. But consider it, my dear friend. I should not want you to miss any potential happiness simply because you have not even thought about the fact that you might be in love with the gentleman."

"In love with him?" Almeria swallowed, those words seeming to burn her lips. "Certainly I cannot be in love with him, Deborah. He and I are like brother and sister. I have told you so many times."

"And yet, consider your response to his absence." Miss Madeley tipped her head, her eyebrow lifting gently. "That is more than a sister might feel for her brother's absence, I can assure you. Besides which, you are *not* brother and sister. You have been known to each other for a long time perhaps, but you are not kin. Mayhap the beginnings of you falling in love with him came many years ago, before you were ever aware of it. And now it has lingered for so long, it has become a part of you without you ever truly being able to decipher what such feelings are." She chuckled softly. "And it has taken a friend's observation to express it to you." Almeria did not know whether to be horrified or relieved at her friend's considerations. There was such a shock there, that she could barely seem to catch her breath. "Come, we will talk of something else and quicken our steps a little, so we do not lose sight of my Mama."

Miss Madeley, perhaps sensing how overwhelmed Almeria felt, began to talk of the upcoming ball. Almeria's head turned as she listened to her friend's delight, only for both shock and overwhelming delight to pour into her, causing her heart to beat furiously at the sight of none other than Lord Coppinger and Lord Trevelyan. They were walking together, with Lord Coppinger's hands clasped neatly behind his back, his head tilted towards his friend. As they spoke, there were no smiles or laughter, but instead, there was a very grave expression on Lord Coppinger's face. All the same, Almeria's heart yearned to hear his voice, and she found herself calling his name before she had even thought to do so. She did not miss the sharp look sent to her by Miss Madeley but dared not look at her directly.

Thankfully, Lord Coppinger looked towards her, and he immediately started forward, only to stop, inclining his head before making to turn away.

"Marcus!" Now her feet were hurrying forward, closing the space between them as Lord Coppinger cleared his throat, with Lord Trevelyan shrugging a little. "How good it is to see you."

"Almeria." He did not smile, and certainly his gaze

would not linger on hers. "Good afternoon."

"Good afternoon." Hearing that she sounded a little breathless, Almeria quickly directed her greeting to Lord Trevelyan, who nodded, but again did not smile. "I have been so eager to see you of late, Marcus." Directing her attention back to her friend, Almeria continued quickly before Lord Trevelyan could say anything. "You have been in society certainly, and we have been at many occasions together, but I have not been able to find the opportunity to talk with you."

Lord Coppinger cleared his throat and his gaze shifted to her left.

"As you know, I am seeking a bride." He offered her a smile, but his eyes did not meet hers. He appeared to be looking somewhere over her shoulder, as though something in the distance was much more interesting. "I am afraid we cannot always be in company; else I would never have occasion to dance or speak with anyone else, and what would be the point in that?"

Almeria blinked, a little surprised at his tone.

"Y... yes, of course." Her delight in seeing him began to blow away, like a candle that had been snuffed out. "But would you not call upon me soon? I am certain that you will be able to spare me a few minutes, surely? Perhaps we could take tea and talk, as we have done so many times before?"

Lord Coppinger shook his head and Almeria's heart tore.

"As I have said, I am very busy becoming better acquainted with various young ladies and I am afraid that I must give all of my time to them." Finally, he looked directly at her but there was no flash of happiness in his eyes. "How is your acquaintance with Lord Penforth proceeding?"

There was a slight curl of his lip as he spoke, and

Almeria caught herself frowning. Something was most concerning here. After all of her years of friendship with Marcus, he had never once before turned down an opportunity to be in company with her, nor had he ever not been able to look into her eyes. What was it that troubled him? Was it because she had long been in company with Lord Penforth? Was that his reason for stepping away?

"I am not certain about continuing my association with Lord Penforth. He has not yet asked to court me, but when he does, I cannot yet state what my answer will be. I am not in love with him and therefore, that shall be the determining factor – although there is time for my feelings to change, of course."

The instant those words left her mouth, Lord Coppinger's gaze shot to hers.

"You... you are not certain?"

His eyebrows lifted and Almeria found herself breathing out slowly.

The difficulty lies with Lord Penforth, then.

"No, I am not," she told him honestly. "It has taken me some weeks to be sure of it, but I do not find myself at all inclined to his company. He may be a quiet gentleman, but he is certainly able to share his *many* opinions with me whenever he wishes... which is very often indeed."

She did not mention to Lord Coppinger the fact that Lord Penforth was still very dismissive of him – becoming almost aggressive in that dismissal. Of late, should she so much as mention Lord Coppinger, Lord Penforth's lip would curl and he would state that he did not think Lord Coppinger as fine a gentleman as she did, and would again remind her of the whispers he had heard which, as yet, he had not shared in their entirety, but which he was desirous to do so. It was becoming rather irritating, to the point that

Almeria now mentioned Lord Coppinger as little as she could in Lord Penforth's company.

"I see."

Seeming to be suddenly lost in thought, Lord Coppinger turned himself, looking completely away from them all – including Lord Trevelyan. Lord Trevelyan made some sort of remark to Miss Madeley and a short conversation took place between them, but Almeria continued to focus her attention on her friend

Growing both concerned and irritated when Lord Coppinger did not make any move to turn back towards her, Almeria chose to act.

"Whatever is the matter, Marcus?"

Stepping closer, she put a hand on his arm, encouraging him to turn around. Immediately Lord Trevelyan and Miss Madeley moved a little away, allowing them to speak freely whilst still being in proper company together. Lord Coppinger looked at her, then shrugged.

"There is nothing the matter."

"Nonsense!" Almeria exclaimed, furiously. "You have been staying so far away from me these last few weeks, I feel it most painfully." The honesty with which she spoke was a familiar one, for she had never held anything back from Lord Coppinger before. Why should she do so now? "If there is something the matter, if there is something I have done which has troubled you so, would you not speak to me of it?" Her hand ran down his arm to his hand but the moment their fingers touched he pulled his away very swiftly indeed. Almeria made to grasp his fingers again regardless, only to realize that she could not be so forward, not when they were in a public setting. Even if Miss Madeley's mother was now standing a short distance away, speaking with her acquaintance, that did not mean that she would not be watching them all carefully. "Speak to me, Marcus," she said, beseechingly. "Why is there such distance between us? What is it that I have done?"

Coughing roughly, he shook his head, barely catching her eye.

"You have done nothing wrong, Almeria."

His low voice sent a pang of longing into her soul, and her breath seemed to catch in her throat as she realized that what Miss Madeley had suggested might very well be true. Could it be that she was in love with Lord Coppinger, her very dearest of friends, the man who had always been a part of her life for so many years? Blinking, she swallowed away her thoughts, then looked at him again.

"Then what is it?"

When he did not answer, Almeria again reached for his hand and this time he did not pull away. Finally his steely grey eyes met hers, but his jaw tightened, and only a short moment later he was already looking past her.

"As I have said, it is quite natural for our friendship to move to another place." Muttering this, he passed one hand over his eyes, as though speaking to her in such a way was painful for him. "I must seek a bride and therefore spend a good deal of my time in that pursuit. If it is not Lord Penforth who will court you, then I am certain that you will have a good many gentlemen seeking to replace him. You shall have to choose wisely."

Almeria's chin wobbled as tears began to prick at the corners of her eyes. This was not the gentleman she knew. This was not Lord Coppinger, as she had always known him. This was someone different; a stranger standing before her, pretending to be the very gentleman she cared for.

"I think you forget how long our friendship has been." Forcing back her tears and murmuring softly, she saw his eyes alight to hers and allowed her fingers to lace through his own, stepping closer so that their grasp would be hidden from any prying eyes. "I can tell when something is troubling you, Marcus. You have never behaved in this manner toward me, and you may give me every excuse that you wish, but I shall not believe it. Something more is occurring, something you do not wish to tell me about, and while I can respect that, I still pray that you might be honest with me. If it is something that I can aid you with in any way, then you know that I would be willing to do it."

"Almeria." Speaking her name so softly, Lord Coppinger looked at her and there was such a sadness in his eyes, Almeria caught her breath. What was the reason for such sorrow? "Would that I could tell you."

The throatiness of his voice made her heart pound with a sudden fear and she squeezed his hand tightly.

"You *can* tell me, Marcus."

Her voice matched his softness, and she moved closer to him still, but Marcus took a step back, dropped his head, and pulled his hand away. When she tried to protest, he simply shook his head.

"It was very good to see you again." His throat bobbed, his grey eyes swirling with dark clouds. "But I fear we cannot ever be as close as we once were, Almeria. Not again."

A sob broke from her lips.

"But what if I should wish it?" Almeria's voice rose a little, desperation twining through her words. "Marcus, my *dear* friend, you cannot simply push our friendship aside, not when we have been so close for so many years. Can you not see how much this pains me? I know it must pain you also." Her eyes searched his, as she held one hand out imploringly to him. "Do you not care?"

In that one moment, something flashed in Lord Coppinger's eyes. Before she knew it, he was beside her, his hand on hers, sparks flashing in his eyes, heat in his cheeks, and his breath warm across her face.

"Of course I care." His voice dropped low as she shuddered, lightly. "That is precisely why I must do this, Almeria. Please do not question me. It is because I care so much for you that I *must* step back, even though it goes against everything I desire."

Almeria caught her breath, her heart beating furiously as her eyes went to his lips. Then her gaze flicked back to his eyes, as she heard his gasp of breath, his own eyes flaring wide. Something warm began to pool in her belly as she reached up her other hand to press lightly to his cheek – only for Lord Coppinger to freeze in place, his gaze now fixed over her shoulder. At the next moment, he turned sharply to Lord Trevelyan, stepping away from her, leaving nothing but cold and shadow in his place.

"We must go."

Not a single word was said to Almeria, not a single explanation given, but without another murmur, both gentlemen turned on their heels and strode sharply away. Almeria stared after them, her breath coming quick and fast as she fought to understand what had just taken place.

"Goodness, that was most abrupt." Miss Madeley blinked in surprise, shaking her head as Almeria glanced over her shoulder. Her breath hitched as none other than Lord Penforth strolled towards them, a broad smile on his face. Her stomach dropped. "I do not understand."

Miss Madeley was about to continue speaking, but Almeria rounded on her friend, reaching out to grasp her hand.

"Do not say it was Lord Coppinger and Lord Trevelyan

with us," she whispered urgently as her friend stared at her, wide-eyed. "Do you understand? We must not say it was Lord Coppinger."

"Say it to whom?"

Almeria tilted her head back.

"To Lord Penforth, for he is approaching us. I am certain that he is the reason Lord Coppinger removed himself from our company so quickly. Please, Deborah, do not say a word about him. If you must, lie, and state instead that it was another fellow altogether."

There was no time for them to say anything more, for Lord Penforth was soon upon them. He bowed to them both and Almeria responded with a quick smile, though her heart was still pounding furiously.

"Good afternoon to you both. Might I ask if I interrupted a conversation? I was sure I saw Lord Coppinger departing from you, along with another companion."

Almeria coughed lightly and attempted to look surprised.

"No indeed, it was not." She spoke quickly, seeing Lord Penforth's smile fade to a sudden frown. "I have not seen my friend in some time. In fact, I was telling Miss Madeley just now that he is no longer in my company as often."

Lord Penforth was not as astute a gentleman as he desired to be, for the smile he attempted to hide was *more* than obvious to Almeria's eyes. He began talking about something entirely different, but in Almeria's heart she believed that what she suspected was true. There was something about Lord Penforth's presence, something about him which was pushing Lord Coppinger away from her... and Almeria was quite certain that Lord Penforth was doing it deliberately.

All she had to do now was find out the truth.

CHAPTER THIRTEEN

*M*arcus could not seem to concentrate on anything. It had been almost four weeks since he had last spoken to Lord Penforth, almost four weeks since he had found himself thrown into a situation of entirely his own making. Of course, Lord Penforth was the one to blame for what *he* had done, but all the same, Marcus could not ignore that, had he told Lady Almeria the truth of his feelings long before now, then they might never have found themselves in this circumstance. Indeed, he might have been quite contented, glad to be with Almeria in society's company, able even to call her his wife, had he been so bold.

Now he must stay away from her, for what could he do against Lord Penforth's threats? It was Marcus' love for Lady Almeria which kept him away from her. Should he say a single word to her, then Lord Penforth would tell nothing but lies about Marcus *and* Lord Trevelyan and with other gentlemen to confirm what Marcus had supposedly been doing in that red-doored gambling den, his reputation would be pulled from him – and Almeria with it. Marcus doubted that he would ever be allowed to even *speak* with her again, should her father hear and believe these whispers, and therefore, he could not allow such a thing to happen.

If he dared speak a word against Lord Penforth, then the heavens would break open, and nothing but fire would rain down upon him. For Marcus, it felt as though he were being slowly pulled into pieces, for every day he was further away from Lady Almeria was a day of pain. What else could he do other than slowly disentangle himself from her? It was not that his thoughts were willing to do so, however, for his mind and his heart were still continually plagued by thoughts of her. Even if Lord Penforth did not manage to secure her hand, it was not as though Marcus could ever find the fulfillment of his heart's greatest longing. He did not doubt that Lord Penforth would be as good as his word, and make certain that Marcus and Lady Almeria were never as Marcus wished them to be. There was a cruelty in him that Marcus disliked immensely, a cruelty that he could practically feel emanating from the gentleman every time Lord Penforth as much as caught his gaze.

Almeria had written him a letter almost daily this last sennight or so. Letters begging him to tell her the truth – but he had not been able to answer. How could he, when he feared what would occur should he do so?

Dropping his head low, he curled one hand into a fist and slammed it down onto the study desk. His hand radiated pain, but he cared very little. It was nothing compared to the sheer agony which stabbed through his heart every time Almeria came to his mind. How much he had lost, how much he had never managed to grasp! And it was all because he had lacked the courage to step forward, all because he had thought to wait until the most favorable moment before he confessed his feelings. He ought to have done so the moment he had laid eyes on her this Season, knowing that the only thing he wanted in his life was her. Now, it was much too late. There was no future for them and all that lay before him was darkness.

"My Lord."

Marcus looked up. His butler had opened the door, and Lord Trevelyan was now pushing past him, stepping inside.

"My apologies, but you may not have heard my knock." Lord Trevelyan dismissed the butler with a wave of his hand. "Coppinger, you have been hiding in here for four days now." Planting both hands on Marcus' desk, he leaned forward, looking him square in the eye. "You cannot simply retreat into your house forever."

"There is no reason for me to be in amongst society," Marcus said. "In fact," he continued, speaking now on impulse, "I think I shall return to my estate."

Lord Trevelyan shook his head and rolled his eyes.

"I hardly think that is a wise idea." With a deep breath, he stood up straight. "I have been considering this, Coppinger, and have decided that we must not allow Lord Penforth to be victorious."

"Then what can I do?" Marcus threw up his hands but remained in his chair. "I cannot see any way out of this situation. I cannot find a way to tell her all that we know of Lord Penforth without injuring her. In many ways, I care very little for myself, but to know her father will pull us apart for what will be the rest of our lives is deeply upsetting." Letting out a long breath he pressed the bridge of his nose lightly. "If they were to become betrothed, then I would, of course, tell her all and then return to my estate, accepting the consequences – but for the moment, I cannot think what else to do. Even if she turns from him, I dare not confess the truth. Penforth would do what he has threatened anyway, out of spite."

"I have been considering it also." Lord Trevelyan began to pace about the room. "I think that you do her a disservice by refusing to allow her to make her own decision."

Marcus blinked.

"A disservice?" This time he did hoist himself out of the chair, but only to make his way to pour two brandies. "I am doing nothing but treating Almeria with the greatest respect and consideration."

Lord Trevelyan smiled and took the offered brandy glass from Marcus.

"I understand that you believe you are doing so." With a shrug, he lifted both shoulders. "But the truth is, you are denying her the chance to hear everything and to make her own decision about it all. After some consideration, I do not think it is fair to her." His lips pulled to one side for a moment. "I saw how troubled she was when you spoke to her some days ago." Recoiling at the memory, Marcus turned away and took a sip of his brandy, praying that the liquor would lessen the pain which continued to shroud him. Lord Trevelyan sighed as Marcus glanced at him. "Forgive me for being so blunt in speaking to you of this. I have found myself quite lost these last few weeks with regard to Lord Penforth's threats, just as you are now."

"Have you thought of the fact that you also could potentially be injured by whatever I say to Lady Almeria?"

Marcus waited for his friend to react, but Lord Trevelyan only shrugged and spoke again.

"That may be so, but mayhap we do not give in to lies. I do not like to be threatened." His jaw clenched suddenly.

"Nor do I like being told that I must stay silent about some evil, simply because of some greater wickedness."

Understanding what his friend meant, Marcus took another sip of his brandy and shook his head, still with a great sense of hopelessness wrapping around his heart.

"What else is there for us to do? If I tell Almeria the truth, then all will be lost. Lord Penforth will tell her, and all who will listen, that he saw me in the gambling den and, no doubt, will make up something utterly awful which he will bandy about society. Thereafter, his friends and companions will attest to it, and society will reject me. I will be pushed even further from Almeria than I already am at present, and that is almost too great a burden for my mind to accept."

Lord Trevelyan nodded slowly but tilted his head.

"Are we not allowing his evil to overcome us then?"

Marcus winced, his whole being rebelling at the idea.

"I do not like it but–"

Lord Trevelyan tilted his head.

"We can fight it."

Taking a moment, Marcus spread out one hand.

"And how precisely are we to do that? If you have a suggestion, I would be glad to hear it." No idea of his own came to his mind, and thus he could only look at Lord Trevelyan, seeing his friend smile and silently praying that somehow, he knew exactly what they could do. "I confess I have very few ideas of my own."

"Then allow me to suggest something for you." Lord Trevelyan grinned. "Perhaps we might find one or two of those gentlemen who were at the same gambling den as Lord Penforth on the night when we stumbled in." Lord Trevelyan paused for a moment, swirling his brandy.

"Mayhap we might offer them something more than Lord Penforth has done."

Considering, Marcus frowned.

"You mean to say that we should bribe them? Threaten them?"

"Bribe, of course." Lord Trevelyan chuckled somewhat wryly. "I can see that the idea does not sit well with you, but it may be our only means to fight back against Lord Penforth's attack."

Considering this, Marcus took in a long breath, letting the air fill his lungs.

"I... I am not certain. I do not want to be a gentleman of disrepute. I do not want to be the same as Lord Penforth."

"I can understand that – but this may be our only opportunity. You *have* to tell Lady Almeria the truth, and we can only do so if we have the assurance that it will be only Lord Penforth to speak against us. If that should happen, I will be able to defend you, and you will be able to defend me. If he does not have the strength of these men behind him, then he has nothing but his own words."

Something shifted in Marcus's spirit, something he could not quite explain, but which was there, nonetheless. It filled his heart and lifted it a little as his eyes went to Lord Trevelyan, his chest suddenly feeling a little looser.

"By doing so, we would take away the strength of his arm."

"Precisely." Lord Trevelyan grinned. "That is exactly what he wants, is it not? Power and control over our actions – but the only way in which he can speak to us with such confidence is because he has great strength behind him. He has those men who will support him in what he says, for they appear to be loyal to him in some way. However, if we were to find a way to make certain that they would align with us, rather than with him, then...."

Slowly, Marcus let the idea settle into his mind and felt his lips curve into the first smile which had crossed his lips in many days.

"Do you know any of the gentlemen? They all stood at a distance from us, and I confess I do not know any of them."

"Fortunately, I do – at least, I think that I recognized one of the gentlemen – a Lord Wilson. It will take a bit of courage on our part, and we will have to speak directly, stating quite clearly what we have seen and what we demand."

"I have lacked courage for far too long." Growing angry with himself and his previous failure to act, Marcus shook his head. "I am sorry for that, old friend – and for my mood at present. I have been lost in the darkness and the shadow, but now I have every intention of doing just as you have suggested. If I am to have any chance of happiness, then you are right, I *should* be seeking every avenue, teasing every path, until we are able to extract ourselves from Lord Penforth's grip."

Lord Trevelyan lifted his glass in a toast.

"You are recovered now, my friend," he replied, quietly. "Now, shall we seek out this gentleman? Or do you wish to hide yourself away in your townhouse for a little longer?"

Marcus grinned back at him.

"I think I am quite tired of my own company. Let us go and seek out this Lord Wilson." Setting down his brandy, he was about to make his way to the door, only for it to suddenly be flung open and, to his utter astonishment, none other than Lady Almeria to tumble into the room. She was entirely alone, and as the door slammed shut behind her,

Marcus caught his breath, stepping towards her. "Almeria! Whatever are you doing here?"

Lord Trevelyan took a small step backward but did not go to the door, turning around instead so that he would not watch their interaction.

"What is it he has done, Marcus?" Almeria's eyes were fixed on his, her hands reaching out to him. "What is it Penforth has done?" Her hand was now pressed against his heart, scrunching lightly into his shirt as her hazel eyes shifted between green and brown. "Please do not pretend any longer. I know that there is something – something which he has done or said to you. For all that I feel, and for all that we have ever shared, please tell me at once what it is. I cannot bear our separation any longer."

A little overwhelmed by her fervency, Marcus took a breath, swallowing hard.

"Almeria, I–"

"Do not push me away." Her fingers pushed a little more against his heart, her voice wobbling with emotion. "I will not leave you until you tell me."

The swell of love in his heart for this young lady had him pressing his hand against hers as it rested lightly over his heart, smoothing out her fingers.

"Almeria."

His voice was a throaty whisper and, from the corner of his eye, Marcus spotted Lord Trevelyan moving toward the window, his hands clasped behind his back, clearly giving them as much privacy as he could while still maintaining propriety – not that there was any true propriety in an unmarried young woman being in a room with two gentlemen!

"Please tell me, Marcus." Almeria's eyes were filled with tears, glistening gently at the edges of her lashes. "I know that you have been staying away from me these last few weeks. I have seen it. I have felt it, *here*." Her other hand pressed against her own heart as tears began to drip onto her cheeks. "And do not give me the excuse that you search for a bride. I will not believe it."

Marcus licked his lips.

"It is true that I have been looking for a bride, Almeria, although not with any great degree of fervency."

She laughed softly, tears splashing down her cheeks.

"Then who have you settled on?" Marcus shook his head, unable to answer. "You see?" Lady Almeria laughed softly. "You cannot even tell me who this lady is. You cannot give me a name because there *is* no young lady you have been pursuing. You may have used that as an excuse previously, but it is not an excuse I believe any longer."

His free hand lifted to push a curl from her face.

"I do not want to injure you, Almeria."

She looked up beseechingly into his face.

"You will not injure me by telling me the truth." There was a softness in her tone, but her cheeks flushed, sending light into her eyes. "I can see that there is another reason for your absence from me, a reason you will not tell me about. I have been upset and confused over it – except that now I know for certain that Lord Penforth has something to do with it all."

"How can you be so certain?"

"Because I saw him speak with you the day that we met in the park. That was the last time we spoke together." Her chin lifted a little. "You made your way from my side abruptly, and it was only when Lord Penforth joined me and asked directly whether or not you had come to speak with me, that I realized the two situations were connected."

With a sigh, Marcus dropped his head forward, his breath hissing out between his teeth.

"I ought to have known that you would find out the truth somehow."

"Except I do not know all of it as yet," Almeria whispered, her fingers trailing lightly across his cheek so that he would lift his head to look at her. "You must speak with me. You must tell me the truth - I beg of you. I do not think that I can live without hearing it from your lips."

There was nothing Marcus could do but tell her all. He knew that she would not leave his side until he had told her. Even if he should lie, he had no doubt that she would know, she would see it in his eyes. With a sigh, he pressed her hand.

"Very well, I shall tell you." Leading her by the hand across the room, he placed her in a chair before sitting next to her, glancing across at Lord Trevelyan and seeing that he still stood by the window, looking out. With a deep breath, Marcus looked straight into her eyes and began. "Yes, this is to do with Lord Penforth. You are right when you say that I did not think him a suitable gentleman for you, although, at the time, I had no particular reason as yet." Choosing to ignore the truth about the bouquets at present, Marcus decided not to discuss his own feelings yet but continued. "I saw Lord Penforth and desired to speak with him. I wanted to make it quite clear that I required him to be worthy of you. You can imagine, to my horror, that as I followed him one evening, I found him making his way to a darker part of London."

"But why were you following him?"

She quite reasonably wanted to know, and Marcus cleared his throat gruffly, quickly searching for an explanation.

"It was my desperation to speak with him that forced my hand." It was not the very best of reasons, but it was a reason, nonetheless – and a true one, in fact – and thankfully, Almeria merely nodded. Briefly, Marcus spoke about what had taken place, told her of Lord Penforth's threats and of the other gentlemen coming to stand behind him. A short while later, he spoke of his anger, his frustration, and his deep regret that he had ever been forced into stepping away from Almeria.

"It was not something which I wanted to do, Almeria. It was something I had no choice but to obey, to protect you."

She reached out one hand to him and Marcus grasped it quickly, praying that she understood.

"I can see that." Her soft smile made his heart throw itself around in his chest. "You did not do so willingly."

Marcus closed his eyes, squeezing them shut for a moment.

"You cannot know how much it has pained me to withdraw from you. I have seen your confusion and felt myself burn with anger over it, but I have done it all to protect you."

"I know." Sitting on the very edge of her chair, Almeria reached out to run her fingers down his cheek. "I can see it in your face, in your eyes. I knew in my heart that you had not pushed away from me simply because you wanted to do so."

A sigh had her dropping her hand, but Marcus' skin was heated as if she had left an imprint upon him, such was the fierceness of the heat which now burned through his frame.

"I must ask you to forgive me."

Looking away, Marcus dropped his gaze for fear his heart would betray him, should he continue to look into her eyes.

"Forgive you?" Almeria repeated, sounding greatly astonished. "Why ever should I have to forgive you?"

"Because I did not fight hard enough to find a way to tell you."

Marcus shrugged a shoulder, not sure where to look, but finding that if he looked into her eyes, his heart beat so furiously, he could barely hear anything save for the blood roaring in his ears.

"What if Lord Penforth had asked to wed me?" Her eyes rounded suddenly. "What would you have done then?"

Marcus scowled.

"I would never have let you marry him, regardless of the consequences. Each day and night were fraught with difficulty, Almeria. I could barely take a breath without thinking of you. Should Lord Penforth have attached himself to you, then I would have done everything in my power to make certain that you knew the truth about his character."

Lady Almeria sighed softly.

"You have always been an excellent gentleman, Marcus. You prove it to me again."

Marcus' heart grew heavy. He did not feel like an excellent gentleman at this moment. He felt as though he were a gentleman who had come close to breaking the most important friendship in his life, simply because he had given up fighting.

"I should have found a way." His eyes looked straight into hers. "I should have found a way to tell you as much as I was able. It has been a difficult circumstance where I have been doing my best to protect you, while being fearful for what the future might hold. I assure you, Almeria, if I had believed that Lord Penforth was about to propose to you, I would have done something – I would have done anything to prevent you from being wed to him, even if it had meant ruining my own reputation."

"That was always his intention." Lord Trevelyan glanced over his shoulder. "I do not mean to interrupt, but only to promise you, Lady Almeria, that Lord Coppinger said so to me on multiple occasions. He stated that, should Lord Penforth so much as begin to court you, he would do whatever was required to make certain that you knew the truth."

This was said with a somewhat pointed look in Marcus's direction, but Marcus ignored it. He did not need to say anything to Almeria about the bouquets, not as yet. There would be time for that later on, but for the moment the only thing required of him was to be truthful about Lord Penforth.

"You feel his threat even now, even though I told you I was not particularly inclined towards him?" Lady Almeria's voice was soft, her eyes still flicking around his face. "Even if I should separate myself from him, which I certainly plan to do, you believe he will carry out his threat?"

"As I have said," Marcus told her, softly, aware of the gentle warmth swirling through him as her thumb ran back and forward over the back of his hand. "I believe that he will do whatever he must to separate you from me. I believe he knows that I..."

Trailing off, Marcus closed his mouth, refusing to state that he loved her. He could not do it, not when she was so upset, when he had already overwhelmed her with the truth about Lord Penforth.

"This cannot be allowed to continue, however." Lord Trevelyan came over to join them. "Lord Penforth cannot simply be allowed to continue in such a way."

"Then you have a plan to remove his threat?"

The heat between them was gone as Marcus looked to Lord Trevelyan and then back to Lady Almeria. Her hand still clasped his, but it was not as tight, her fingers not seeking to lace through his own. Sighing softly, he nodded.

"That is our intention." Seeing her eyes flare, he tilted his head to Lord Trevelyan. "It was Lord Trevelyan's thought. He thinks we should find the gentlemen whom Lord Penforth surrounded himself with, and demand that they show loyalty to us rather than to him."

Lady Almeria caught her breath. Her mouth was a round circle, and her eyes flared.

"And how will you make that demand?"

Leaning forward, Marcus settled his hand atop their joined ones so that she could look directly into his face.

"We will not threaten, but we may bribe. We would not ever do something as cruel as Lord Penforth has done to us, but there must be a way to demand their loyalty. It may take a great deal of coin, perhaps even a favor or two, but if it can be done, then we must try."

Lady Almeria took in a deep breath, nodding slowly.

"I can see your reasoning, but what happens if they cannot be bought? Then what will you do?"

Courage built like a fire in his chest as he held her gaze.

"Then I will tell the truth," he said honestly. "And I will tell it in front of as many of the *ton* as will listen. I have no doubt that Lord Penforth will then gather his friends and have them refute everything which I have said, but I shall have Lord Trevelyan, and I also have my reputation. Perhaps combined, both will be enough to protect me."

Fresh tears clung to Almeria's eyes but she nodded, sniffing lightly.

"And you shall have me, Marcus," she murmured as Lord Trevelyan tactfully turned his back again. "I have no

interest in Lord Penforth, not in any way. I have no enjoyment in his company. I find him to be arrogant and conceited." She took a deep breath and then looked back at Marcus
steadily. Something formed in Marcus' stomach like a
coiling snake, ready to strike, his heart beating painfully
again. "And besides which, I do not love him. He may claim
to love me, but I do not think that his form of love is one I
want in my life."

"No, he does not love you." The words were pouring
from a place deep within himself, no longer held back. "I
know what love is, Lady Almeria. I know what it feels like
to be so lost in love that one can barely think! I know how
it is when a single word, a single look from the object of
one's affection is so overpowering, it makes the entire day
seemed to fill with bright sunshine. But at the same time,
it dazzles one greatly, one cannot look anywhere else. I
know the depth of love that sends a craving, clawing
hunger into one's soul, desperate for it to be satisfied,
furious with a hunger for words of affection to be spoken
in return. No, Lord Penforth does not love you, Almeria.
He may state that he does, but I have no doubt that it is a
lie. He seeks you only because of who you are and
because of what you can offer him. I know that for
certain."

Lady Almeria's eyes flared, but she said nothing, the
only sound in the room was his own quickened breath. Did
she realize the significance of what he had said? Did she
understand that he was speaking of her and what she meant
to him?

"I..." Almeria trailed off into silence and then threw a
glance to Lord Trevelyan. She took another breath and then
rose from her chair, letting his hands go. "I should return to
Lady Yardley. She is waiting for me in the carriage." She

gave him a brief smile. "I am grateful to her for her trust in me, but I can't ask her to linger too long."

Feeling as though another moment had been snatched from him, Marcus rose to his feet.

"Almeria, if you would only wait but another moment, I –"

"I shall remain close to Lord Penforth, for the moment."

Almeria looked from Lord Trevelyan to Marcus, and back again, and as his friend ambled towards him, Marcus had to accept the moment was truly gone.

"I... yes, I suppose you should."

There seemed to be nothing else to say. The chance to reveal his own heart would come again another time.

"Yes, we want him to think that all is well," Lord Trevelyan confirmed as Lady Almeria nodded, looking anywhere but Marcus' face. "And when we have been able to speak with Lord Wilson – the gentleman I believe was present that evening – we will be able to make a plan for what will come."

"A plan I am to be included in."

Lady Almeria lifted an eyebrow as she finally caught his gaze, offering him a small smile.

"Yes, of course." Marcus murmured his agreement, his emotions rising into a great swell before crashing down over him. How much he wanted to say and how little he had the opportunity to speak! "Allow me to accompany you back to Lady Yardley."

Marcus hurried forward, but Almeria only smiled and shook her head.

"There is no need." She put one hand on his arm, but her eyes sank to the floor. "I am sorry to have pushed in here in such an unruly fashion. Thank you for telling me every-thing, Marcus. I am grateful."

Entirely frustrated over what might have taken place within these last few minutes had not Lord Trevelyan been present, Marcus smiled lightly and then nodded.

"But of course. I will write to you soon, once we know where the meeting with Lord Wilson is to be."

"Thank you, Marcus."

Instead of looking at him, smiling, or even embracing him, Almeria simply turned away, leaving Marcus to watch after her until the door closed behind her, leaving him with a mixture of frustration and relief within his heart.

CHAPTER FOURTEEN

"There is something I must tell you all." Almeria lifted her chin and looked around the room at all of her friends. "Lord Penforth is not a gentleman of fine character."

This news brought some dramatic gasps from Miss Millington, and also from Lady Shelbourne, but Lady Yardley did not appear at all surprised. Instead she simply nodded, her eyes remaining steady as she looked at Almeria.

"I knew something was wrong the moment that Lord Coppinger hastened to leave my side when Lord Penforth approached myself and Miss Madeley, only last week." She looked to Miss Madeley who nodded in firm agreement, quickly recalling how startled they had been to see his firm but hasty departure, and Lord Penforth's questions thereafter as to whether or not it had been Lord Coppinger who had been speaking with them. Nodding to Miss Madeley in thanks, Almeria continued as her friends looked back at her. "I asked Lady Yardley if we might stop for a brief visit to Lord Coppinger's townhouse on our way here, and she was kind enough to agree. After speaking with Lord Trevelyan and Lord Coppinger, I am now very well aware that there is something most unsavory about Lord Penforth's character. I say this so that you will all make certain to remain far from him. I have no intention of lingering close to him at all."

Miss Madeley let out a long, audible breath.

"And I, for one, am very pleased to hear it," she remarked, bringing a little levity to the room as some of the young ladies smiled. "I confess that I do not much like Lord Penforth at this moment – in fact, I have not liked him very much at all, from the very beginning of our acquaintance!"

Even Almeria managed to laugh at this, nodding her head as her friends looked around the room, murmuring to each other.

"Would you like to tell us what has taken place?" Lady Yardley reached out and squeezed Almeria's hand for a moment. "When you came back to the carriage, you did look very pale, though something was shining in your eyes which had not been there before."

Smiling softly, Almeria ignored the lump in her throat.

"The light was there because I finally learned the truth. I see now that Lord Coppinger has done his best to protect me from being surrounded by evil. Lord Penforth has attempted to blackmail him, for Lord Coppinger followed him one night, determined to speak to Lord Penforth about his acquaintance with me. To his horror, he discovered that Lord Penforth went to a gambling den in the East End of London - a most concerning place from his description! Once Lord Coppinger stepped inside, with his friend Lord Trevelyan, Lord Penforth saw them. He stated that should Lord Coppinger say a word about Lord Penforth's presence there, and whatever it was he was doing in a small private room within that place, then Lord Coppinger's name would be attached to it also. In fact, Lord Penforth threatened that he would say whatever untruths he wished about Lord Coppinger and Lord Trevelyan and would have his words confirmed by some friends, who were also with him that night, although I do not think that Lord Coppinger or Lord Trevelyan recognized them all."

There was a brief silence before a quiet murmur of shock ran around the room.

"This proves that not every gentleman is as he appears." Lady Yardley's voice held a warning. "I am very glad that you were considerate in your acquaintance with Lord Penforth, for it seems that you are clear in your mind about him. In fact, I believe you had already made your decision about him before speaking to Lord Coppinger this afternoon."

"Certainly I had." Almeria lifted her chin, looking again to Miss Madeley who returned her look with a smile. "There is no love in my heart for Lord Penforth. I have given him the opportunity to try to steal my heart, have given him the opportunity to prove his supposed affection for me – but now, upon considering what I feel, I find I am... rather disdainful of him. If I am to be honest, I do not like the gentleman. As I have said, he may claim to have a great affection for me, and he continues to send bouquets, but I take no pleasure in his company."

"Which is quite understandable!" Lady Elizabeth spoke up first. "How very distressing for you to have found all of this out, Almeria. Might I ask what you now intend to do? You say that you will stay far from Lord Penforth, but does that mean his threats will then lessen against Lord Coppinger and Lord Trevelyan?"

Almeria shook her head.

"I cannot be certain, but I am afraid that they will not. For whatever reason, Lord Penforth seems quite determined to push Lord Coppinger away from me. However, I am determined not to allow him to do so – and also to assist Lord Coppinger in doing what I can to prove Lord Penforth's character to society. They shall both see that my determination is just as great as theirs, even though I am a mere woman."

She said this with a wry smile, and some of her friends chuckled while Miss Madeley frowned, clearly aware of her ongoing concern about Lord Penforth.

"Let us hope that you succeed." Miss Madeley caught Almeria's gaze. "What is to happen next?"

"Lord Coppinger and Lord Trevelyan are to speak with a gentleman they believe to have been present the night Lord Penforth threatened them. I should like to be there also."

"Well, there is no reason for you not to be," Lady Yardley stated, with a smile. "If you wish to discover the truth, then I would be glad to accompany you at the time of the meeting. They could not refuse if I am to be there also."

Almeria smiled at the lady.

"Thank you, Lady Yardley. I will send word to Lord Coppinger that you will be present, so that he might inform me of when this meeting will take place."

"You may use my writing desk if you wish," Lady Sherbourne offered as Almeria rose from her chair. "It is through in the small parlor."

"I thank you. I shall do so ."

Quickly, Almeria stepped from the room, only to glance behind her and see that Miss Madeley had come to join her.

"I hope you do not mind if I accompany you?"

Almeria offered her friend a smile as the young woman fell into step beside her.

"No, of course not. Do you wish to join me also, when I attend that meeting with Lord Coppinger?"

Almeria felt a little confused as to her friend's presence – for she was well able to write a letter to Lord Coppinger on her own - and she blinked as her friend laughed softly.

"No, it is not that." Stepping into the parlor, Miss Madeley put one hand on Almeria's arm. "I wanted a private moment to ask you something."

Almeria frowned.

"Something about Lord Coppinger?"

"Yes." Hesitating, Miss Madeley bit the edge of her lip before she continued. "I have wondered whether or not you have noticed the very same about Lord Coppinger as I."

A slight frown crossed Almeria's face.

"I do not think I know what you mean."

Miss Madeley tilted her head, her eyes sharp.

"I initially noticed it some time ago, when you were first seeking out who had sent you those bouquets. I believe it was when Lord Penforth had come to inform you that *he* was the one who had offered them."

Still having very little understanding of what her friend meant, Almeria nodded slowly.

"I recall how angry Marcus was."

"But do you recall something else?" Miss Madeley lifted her eyebrow. "Did you note how he mentioned, when speaking to Lord Penforth, that you had received *two* types of flowers in your most recent bouquet?"

Resisting the urge to throw up her hands and exclaim that such a thing was of no consequence, Almeria took a breath.

"Of course, I recall such a thing – but what of it? I would have mentioned to him that I had received both roses and tulips, I am sure."

Miss Madeley grinned.

"But what if you had not?"

Blinking, Almeria's lips twisted as she considered.

"Well, if I had not, then I would think –" In an instant, what Miss Madeley was suggesting flung itself so hard at her that she recoiled, stepping backward toward the door, her hands lifting as though she were to defend herself. "No." Her breathing was coming quickly, her heart beating in a furious rhythm as her eyes fixed themselves on her friend. "No, it cannot be. I do not think he..." Trailing off, she considered what Lord Coppinger had said to her on previous occasions, how he had looked at her, how he had smiled with that softness about his eyes. Could it be that *he* had been the one to send her those bouquets? "You are not suggesting that he..."

Still struggling to accept what was being said, she looked long and hard at Miss Madeley, who, after a moment, nodded slowly with a slight smile on her face.

"As hard as it may be to believe, yes, that is precisely what I am suggesting." Taking a moment, she put one hand on Almeria's arm, her eyes searching hers. "I know it must be greatly astonishing to hear me put forward such a thing, but would it not explain his utter vehemence when Lord Penforth confessed the supposed truth to you? Would it not explain why he was so very angry?"

Almeria could do nothing but stare at her friend. It was the most extraordinary thing to even contemplate! And yet, the more she thought of it, the more it seemed to be a possibility. Why, she had never even *allowed* herself to think of the possibility! These last few weeks, all she had considered was how lost she was in her confusion over what she felt about Lord Coppinger and, thereafter, she had become tangled in all Lord Penforth was laying upon her. But what if, in the midst of all of that, Lord Coppinger was simply standing, waiting and watching, looking at her with the love she had been seeking for so long?

"Ohhh..."

"I do hope that I have not shocked you too much." Miss Madeley gave her a small smile. "I felt it my duty to share it with you. That is not to say that I am correct, however. There is always the possibility that I could be wrong but—"

"You are not mistaken," Almeria spoke quickly, putting one hand over her eyes, her whole body suddenly caught with a tremble. "Good gracious, I have never so much as imagined that such a thing could happen! I have always considered him my friend, but perhaps in the midst of all of this, he has been looking at me with an entirely different view. As you have said, this might be why he was so against Lord Penforth, even from the very beginning."

She shivered lightly, recalling just how her heart had leaped upon seeing him as he had come to greet her that night of the ball. How much she had missed him – and how much she yearned for him now.

Miss Madeley laughed softly.

"My dear friend, I am certain that Lord Coppinger would have disliked any gentleman who sought to court you! He would not have shown even the slightest inclination towards him because of his own unexpressed feelings."

A laugh escaped from Almeria's lips, her face warming.

"Good gracious, what a fool I have been. I have been confused and mystified as to why my heart pounds so ridiculously when he is nearby. I have been all of a flutter, become overly distracted and, all in all, have struggled to comprehend myself. It is as though, in his absence these last few years, I have found my heart changing. Yes, he is a dear friend, but what if he has become more than that to me?"

Grinning, Miss Madeley's eyes danced.

"What if, my dear friend, you have done the very worst of things and fallen in love with him? Would that not explain to you why you find yourself so earnestly *against* introducing him to me, why you dislike the idea of one of your friends becoming betrothed to him?"

Her breath spiraled in her chest, her eyes widening as she stared back at Miss Madeley. Surely it could not be? Yes, she cared for him but... was she in love with him? Closing her eyes, she waved one hand in her friend's direction.

"It is not that I was disinclined towards any of you, but only that I.... that I..." Coming to a stuttering stop, she groaned and put both hands to her face. "I did not say a word about my disinclination to anyone. How did you know of it?"

Her friend trilled a laugh.

"Almeria, we have been friends for some years. I am very well able to tell when you are averse to something. You have a slight tilt of your lips that pushes them to a slant and, while you then go on to force a smile, it does not light your eyes. Your expression is always that way whenever you are not particularly enamored of an idea. I saw it when Lady Yardley mentioned introducing Lord Coppinger to your friends who still sought a husband. It was as though you did not want any of us to come close to him."

"That is because it is precisely what I was feeling." Shaking her head to herself, Almeria let out a broken laugh. "It is ridiculous, is it not? I could not understand why I was feeling such a thing, but now I see it. Now I realize that it is simply because I do not want Lord Coppinger to be courting any other young lady... but me."

Her voice softened as she finished the sentence, the

revelation so utterly astonishing that it took Almeria some moments to compose herself. It was as if she were walking into a place of bright sunshine but the light was so very vivid, it was overwhelming. She had never considered this before. Yes, they were the very best of friends, but that did not mean that her consideration of him could not change. It explained everything, explained why she had been so averse to even her friends becoming acquainted with him, for fear that one of them might then end up becoming betrothed to him.

She closed her eyes and shook her head, her lips curving gently.

"Do you know that I had an imagining where I saw you standing up in church with Lord Coppinger?" Opening her eyes, she smiled at Miss Madeley's obvious surprise. "You cannot imagine how distressed I was at it, and then how distressed I was over my strange reaction! But then things became all the more confusing as regards Lord Penforth, and I suppose that I have put such thoughts to the back of my mind."

"No doubt helped by the fact that none of us have been courted by your Lord Coppinger," Miss Madeley quipped, with a chuckle. "Do you recall how furiously you responded to him when he mentioned Miss Tennant? I do not think I have ever seen your eyes flash with such fury!"

Almeria closed her eyes, smiling.

"Oh, pray do not embarrass me! I am already mortified to realize how little I know myself."

"Pray do not be so." Miss Madeley squeezed her hand but looked away, speaking quietly now. "I think love often disguises itself within us. Thus far I have seen three of my friends fall in love, and two of them are now married. I fully expect that you should be the third, of course, but all the same, I have recognized now that love does not come upon everyone in the same way. For some, it appears as a surprise, for others, it takes time to build, and for some...." Her gaze went back to Almeria, her smile, gentle. "For some, it has always been there, lying hidden and undiscovered. But now it has been unearthed, I am certain that you will think it the greatest treasure you have ever possessed."

CHAPTER FIFTEEN

"*Y*ou are aware that Lady Almeria intends to be with us?"

Lord Trevelyan shot Marcus a frown.

"I do not think that wise. I know that she asked to be so, but I did not think that we had agreed upon her presence here."

Marcus grinned.

"Regardless, she will be here within the next few minutes." Seeing his friend shake his head, he shrugged. "I am sure that you can understand that she is deeply engaged in this matter, particularly as regards Lord Penforth, so I did not want to refuse her. Lady Yardley will be present also, although I think that is mostly for propriety."

Lord Trevelyan's frown lingered.

"I suppose she wants to hear exactly what Lord Penforth said to Lord Wilson." He sighed and shook his head. "Though I pray that she will not speak too openly, for it might discourage Lord Wilson from speaking honestly with us if she were to ask too many questions. From what I know of Lady Almeria, she is quite determined."

"She can be," Marcus smiled to himself, "but that is one of her finest qualities. She has known from the very beginning what it was that she sought in her marriage. She wanted a gentleman who would love her, and I am very glad to know that Lord Penforth is not such a gentleman."

"But you are." Lord Trevelyan chuckled, his frown gone. "You *are* going to tell her very soon about the bouquets, I assume?"

Marcus nodded and was about to say more, only for the door to open and the butler to step inside. He was followed thereafter by Lady Yardley and Lady Almeria – and also by Lord Wilson.

"We arrived together." Lady Yardley offered a brief smile to Lord Wilson who returned it, although Marcus noticed the flash of confusion in his eyes. "I assured Lord Wilson that we were meant to be present with you."

"I did not think we would be taking tea together."

Lord Wilson was a slightly older man with shoulders which rounded a little, a wobble about his jaw, and greying hair which was already slightly receding. Marcus did not recognize him, but from the look on Lord Trevelyan's face, it seemed that he did.

"We are not about to take tea together, I am afraid." Speaking quickly as the butler stepped outside, he nodded as Lord Trevelyan made his way towards the door, standing in front of it so that Lord Wilson could not easily make an escape. "We are here, in fact, to speak to you about another matter. A matter which concerns Lady Almeria also."

Lord Wilson's gaze traveled towards the two ladies.

"I do not want to say anything which will have society whisper about me." His chin wobbled. "I know very well that Lady Yardley writes the London Ledger. I have no desire for my sins to be published for all of society to chew upon."

Sins? Marcus blinked in confusion, rubbing one hand over his chin. He had no knowledge of what the gentleman referred to, and despite Lady Yardley's profound reassurances she had no intention of doing anything of the sort, Lord Wilson seemed most reluctant. He refused the offer of a brandy, and only sat down in a chair after much encouragement – and thereafter, only sat on the very edge of it, his eyes looking towards the door as though he was eager to make his escape at any available moment. Marcus watched him carefully, for this was not at all what he had expected. He had thought Lord Wilson's demeanor would be one of confidence, that he might come swaggering into the room, delighting in all Lord Penforth had done in proving himself to have so much power Instead, he seemed gravely concerned for some reason – and what sins was it that he was speaking of?

"You are aware of why we wish to speak to you, I am sure." Lord Trevelyan took a step towards Lord Wilson, clasping his hands behind his back. "You saw both myself and Lord Coppinger one night some time ago. It is *that* night which we wish to speak of."

Lord Wilson threw up his hands and made to get out of his chair.

"And I have told you, I have no desire to speak of my sins! Why you thought it would be encouraging to have Lady Yardley present, I can have no idea! I shall take my leave."

"I can assure you I have no intention of putting anything in 'The London Ledger'." Lady Yardley rose from her chair. Even though she was not an overly tall woman, she radiated confidence and authority, for she put one hand on Lord Wilson's arm and led him back to his chair, and the man went as though he were an obedient child. "Now, Lord Wilson, you know that I am an honorable woman and that I always state quite plainly what it is that I have written in the Ledger, whether it be rumor or truth. Therefore, you may have my word that I will not write a single thing about this conversation in my little publication."

Lord Wilson scowled, though he did remain in his chair.

"Then why are you here?" Lady Yardley immediately gestured to Lady Almeria and Marcus watched as the gentleman's eyes flicked towards her. Thereafter, there came a frown billowing across his forehead. "I do not understand." Rather uncomfortable, Lord Wilson let his gaze travel from one side of the room to the other. "I have no comprehension of what it is that you wish to discuss, and I find myself somewhat ill at ease."

"As well you should be," Marcus answered, folding his arms across his chest and glaring at the man, refusing to believe his words. "What you have done in siding with Lord Penforth has brought both myself and Lord Trevelyan a great deal of trouble. It is clear to me that Lord Penforth cannot be called a gentleman and therefore, I am deeply astonished to hear that a gentleman such as yourself, with such a strong family name and excellent reputation, would be so willing as to follow him."

Lord Wilson blinked furiously, then ran one hand over his forehead.

"I do not understand."

Believing this to be entirely fabricated, Marcus rolled his eyes and snorted loudly.

"There is no need to pretend, Lord Wilson. Lord Trevelyan and I were both present the night you saw us speaking with Lord Penforth in that gambling den. We saw your face as you saw ours. I have no doubt that you heard Lord Penforth's declaration and, given that we have had no choice but to obey for fear of what he would do to our reputations, we have found ourselves greatly distressed. What say you to that?"

Lord Wilson's eyes opened wide, and he stared at Marcus as though he had told the most unbelievable tale. After a moment, he shook his head.

"Do you think that I am a friend to Lord Penforth?" His voice was quiet, rasping gently. "I can assure you, gentlemen, that Lord Penforth is *not* the sort of gentleman I wish to associate myself with. It is unfortunate that I have to, certainly, but that is only because we have all been as foolish as each other."

Throwing a look to Lord Trevelyan, Marcus' lips twisted.

He will deny everything. There is no good in speaking with him.

"Might I interject?" Lady Almeria's gentle tones broke through the blossoming silence. "Are you stating, Lord Wilson, that you are not warmly acquainted with Lord Penforth?" Lord Wilson nodded fervently. "And might I ask, are you at all aware of Lord Penforth's threats to Lord Coppinger and Lord Trevelyan, to which you are now associated?" Lord Wilson gasped aloud. His hands grasped the arms of his chair and his eyes flared wide, fixing themselves to Lady Almeria. "I presume you are not."

Lady Almeria looked to Marcus, who immediately began to frown. Had he somehow been mistaken about all of this?

"A threat?" Lord Wilson pulled out a handkerchief and rubbed it liberally over his face. "You believe that I have somehow been involved in a threat against you? That I have been doing Lord Penforth's bidding?"

Marcus' belief that this gentleman knew precisely what Marcus had been threatened with quickly died away. No gentleman could have such a raw response as this and be lying, he was sure of it.

"Perhaps I was mistaken." He offered a brief smile to Lord Wilson, then looked to Lord Trevelyan. "Forgive me, we were both sure that you had aligned yourself with Lord Penforth."

"I have done no such thing." Lord Wilson scowled. "The reason I was near Lord Penforth that night, the reason for my presence in that place at all, was simply because we all had to make our payments, and we then intended to take our leave. We thought we should all go together, you see, for fear that some of us might have been attacked, had we gone alone." Lord Wilson was speaking urgently now, leaning so close to the edge of this chair, it looked as though he might fall from it at any moment. "I am greatly distressed to hear that you believe I was involved in a matter pertaining to that gambling den and Lord Penforth. Not only I, but some other fellows also!"

There came a few moments of pause as Lord Wilson looked around the room, his head twisting one way and then the other as if he fought for them to believe him.

"Might I ask if you could explain your situation from the very beginning?" Lady Almeria tilted her head a little, smiling. "You need not tell us in particular detail if you do not wish it."

Again, her voice offered a moment of pause. She smiled warmly and even Marcus felt himself breathe a little more easily. Her calm tones seemed to encourage Lord Wilson, for he closed his eyes, took a breath, and nodded.

"It is to my shame, my Lady." His face flushed. "I am utterly ashamed of what has taken place, and of how stupidly I have behaved. One evening, at the start of the Season, some gentlemen friends and I were involved in a game of cards. This soon led to a trip to the darker side of London and it was there, unfortunately, where we all lost a great deal of money."

"To whom?" Marcus asked, but Lord Wilson merely shook his head.

Biting his lip, he turned his head away and for a moment, Marcus feared that the man would not speak any further, only for Lord Wilson to sigh heavily again.

"I shall not state his name. I do so in order to protect myself rather than to deliberately frustrate you, which I hope you understand." Clearing his throat, he kept his gaze away from Marcus, clearly ashamed of what he had done. "What I shall tell you is this: given that so many of us had lost a great deal and owed a significant amount, we all agreed that we would return together on a particular day and pay what was owed."

Becoming more and more astonished with every word which Lord Wilson expressed, Marcus ran one hand over his face, attempting to grasp what was being told to him.

"So are you stating that you went to the red-doored gambling den to pay your debts? Lord Penforth also?"

Lord Wilson looked straight at him.

"Precisely. Lord Penforth owed a large amount of coin also, which certainly is not the first of his debts." He shuddered and grimaced. "And I should be glad never to darken the door of that establishment again. Indeed, I have made a silent vow never to lose myself in liquor in such a way ever again, for fear that I will behave with such foolishness that I will lose the entirety of my fortune!"

Lord Trevelyan let out a low whistle, making Lord Wilson looked towards him sharply.

"Then you have no knowledge of what Lord Penforth said to myself and Lord Coppinger as regards Lady Almeria?"

Lord Wilson shook his head, beads of sweat beginning to form on his forehead.

"None whatsoever." He held up both hands as though he would not be believed. "When both myself and the other gentlemen saw you standing there, we chose not to step forward out of naught but shame. I see that my face was not particularly well hidden by the shadows, however."

Marcus could hardly believe what he was hearing. Everything Lord Penforth had thrown at them, every strand of strength he had wound about himself, was nothing more than a pretense. He had been pretending that he had great power when he actually had none at all – and like a fool, Marcus had believed him without question.

"Then Lord Penforth has nothing." Closing her eyes and smiling softly to herself, Lady Almeria let out a quiet sigh. "He cannot make any threats. He has nothing by which he can hold you to, Marcus."

On hearing this, Lord Wilson spread out his hands.

"I am sorry if anything I have done has added to your difficulties."

"Not in the least." Marcus quickly pushed aside his surprise to acknowledge what Lord Wilson had done. "You have caused no difficulties. Instead, you have done a great deal to aid us."

Scowling, Lord Wilson looked away.

"I do not see how telling you of my darkest deeds could be of any use to you."

"It is because of what you have told us of Lord Penforth.

You have revealed a great truth and taken away a heavy burden." Again, Lady Almeria's voice was soft and as Marcus watched, Lord Wilson looked up at her and, much to Marcus' surprise, managed a brief smile. No matter what Lady Almeria said, it seemed she had a way to catch the attention of Lord Wilson, able to speak directly to him in a way that even Marcus could not. "Obviously I will not go into particulars, but needless to say, Lord Penforth has caused a great deal of difficulty for Lord Coppinger and Lord Trevelyan. You have released them from that."

"That is true, Lord Wilson." Marcus managed a smile. "With you telling us the truth of the situation, we are now able to speak to Lord Penforth in a way which we were not able to, before. We will be able to tell him, now, that we know he has no strength, that his threats are empty, and thus, his confidence will surely fade away."

At this, Lord Wilson nodded, but then rose from his chair, clearly unwilling to linger.

"For that, I am grateful – though might you excuse me now? Unless you have any further questions, my shame pushes me to the door."

Rising, Marcus offered his hand to the man and Lord Wilson shook it firmly, though with his other hand he mopped at his forehead again.

"I am truly grateful," Marcus told him. "You have my word that none of what you have divulged to us will be spoken of to anyone else."

Lord Wilson let out a slow breath and nodded, glancing at Lady Yardley, who merely smiled as though to confirm that yes, she would keep her word also.

"Then I bid you all good afternoon."

Without another word, or so much as a glance at any one of them, Lord Wilson left the drawing room, leaving

Marcus to stand directly facing Lady Almeria. His eyes caught hers, and he could not look away. There was nothing between them any longer, nothing that could hold him back, nothing to prevent him from drawing close – if only she would let him.

"I can hardly believe this." Lord Trevelyan shook his head, then ran one hand over his eyes. "How could we have been so foolish, Coppinger? Why did we never consider that Lord Penforth might be lying?"

Rising, he began to pace about the room, forcing Marcus' attention away from Lady Almeria.

"I would not say that you are foolish." Lady Yardley tipped her head, smiling. "It is not foolishness to take a threat seriously, particularly after what you had witnessed."

Marcus smiled rather grimly.

"I admit to being deeply surprised by Lord Penforth's behavior. I thought him just a quiet sort of fellow, only to realize much too late that he was not the sort of character I wished to have anywhere near me. You cannot imagine my horror to discover how selfish he has been – and how calculating."

Lady Almeria smiled at him.

"Thankfully, Lord Wilson has managed to betray Lord Penforth entirely! I confess I look forward to telling Lord Penforth that I have set against accepting his offer of courtship. I have not, of course, ended our connection as yet, but I have every intention of doing so now."

Lady Yardley chuckled, seeming quite pleased with this remark as Marcus let out a sigh of relief that he could not hold back. Lady Almeria's eyes met his and the smile she shared with him was something so meaningful, it sent a flood of warmth to envelop him. Blowing out another long breath, Lady Almeria giggled and looked away, her cheeks now a gentle pink.

"I suppose the next question is - what you plan to do as regards Lord Penforth?" Lady Yardley looked first at Marcus and then at Lord Trevelyan. "Do you intend to simply continue on as though his threat is no longer viable? Or will you say something more to him, to make him clearly aware that he cannot do such a thing to anyone else in the future?"

Marcus considered for a full moment, looking toward Lord Trevelyan and seeing his friend grin.

"He certainly is a darkly calculating fellow. I do not feel it would be right to simply allow society to continue to think well of him when he is nothing but a scoundrel."

"I will confess that I was taken in by him." Lady Almeria suddenly frowned, her smile dropping away. "I did not think he was in any way cruel, but see how wrong I was?"

"You were not the only one Almeria." Lady Yardley pointed one finger towards herself. "I have not heard a single bad word about him. He has hidden his true character very well from all of us, has he not?"

"Which makes it all the more desirous for us to speak openly to society." Looking at Lady Yardley, Marcus took a breath. "And I think I have an idea. Lady Yardley, you will need to be present also, if you do not mind when the time comes for me to speak to Lord Penforth." He glanced at Lord Trevelyan. "And you also, of course."

"Do not think that I will be absent from this." Lady Almeria rose from her chair and came directly towards Marcus, taking his hand in hers even though they were standing in front of Lady Yardley and Lord Trevelyan. Her chin tilted, her hazel eyes suddenly darkening. "I will not be absent from anything concerning Lord Penforth, I want very much to show him that I am no longer taken in by him and that my dislike of him is well founded."

"I quite understand." Smiling at her, Marcus waited until the shadows fell from her eyes as he squeezed her hand, wishing desperately that they were alone so that he might tell her about the bouquets, might confess his love for her. "Yes, you may be present and thereafter, once the matter is at an end, would you be willing to walk in the park with me? There is more I should like to say to you."

Her eyes flared but her smile grew quickly.

"I should be glad to speak with you also, Marcus," she murmured, and Marcus' heart beat furiously with a flurry of hope. Perhaps there might be a joyous ending to the Season after all.

CHAPTER SIXTEEN

"There you are, Penforth. Hiding in the shadows, are you?"

Marcus watched as the gentleman's eyes flickered, his lip curling in an obvious expression of dislike.

"Coppinger." Lord Penforth twisted his head so that he looked away. "I do not think that we have much to say to each other unless it is that you wish to come and congratulate me?"

This time, Marcus lifted an eyebrow.

"Congratulate you?"

Chuckling, Lord Penforth grinned.

"Have you not heard? I am soon to ask Lady Almeria's father, the very excellent Lord Fairburn, whether or not he will permit me to court his daughter."

The urge to laugh and tell Lord Penforth that there was very little hope of him succeeding was strong, but Marcus instead dropped his head, forcing himself to remain stoic. It was not yet time to reveal the truth, and the requirement for him to look sorrowful and beaten down was important.

"I am quite certain that, come the end of the Season, I

will be wed to the beautiful Lady Almeria." Lord Penforth grinned and tilted his head back in a prideful manner as the soiree continued all around them. "I think her the most beautiful, elegant, and articulate creature I have ever met. She is also very willing to listen to me and spends a great deal of time in my company. She remains so very quiet because she is rapt with fascination for my words – a quality I confess I find very pleasing indeed."

Try as he might, Marcus could not hide a snort of laughter, although he quickly covered this by ducking his head and pulling out his handkerchief to pretend to rub his nose. Lord Penforth was nothing but conceited, and yet, at this juncture, it was precisely what Marcus needed. The gentleman had to ooze confidence, to believe himself already victorious if they were to convince him to have another conversation. It did not seem to take a great deal to make Lord Penforth behave so, however, which again, was to Marcus' advantage. Arrogance was a part of Lord Penforth's character, and a most disagreeable feature, as far as Marcus was concerned.

"If I am making you uncomfortable then pray, do tell me." Lord Penforth snorted, still grinning. "Though I cannot promise that I shall stop speaking of my victory – for I will admit aloud that it is pleasing for me to see you so. It makes me all the more delighted with my connection to Lady Almeria!" His grin grew ever wider, his eyes dancing with obvious pride. "Why is it that you so severely dislike my connection to Lady Almeria? Surely you must believe I have some fine qualities since she is clearly so enamored of me? Or is it that jealousy burns within you, and you find yourself painfully rejected?" His chest puffed out, his smile turning dark. "I am *deeply* sorry that you feel so burdened over the matter, but that is the state of things.

You cannot expect her to ever come back to you, to return to the connection as it was. That is gone forever, and she is quite lost to you. That is simply something you must accept."

Marcus could only nod slowly, choosing not to say anything, and remain silent as Lord Penforth continued. Anger blossomed at the man's conceit, but he held it within himself as Lord Penforth continued with his extensive explanation of why he was the most suitable of all gentlemen for Lady Almeria, of how much she admired him, and how often they spent time together. Marcus listened, taking in deep breaths and letting the air out again slowly so that he would keep his temper in check. How much he longed to throw everything back in Lord Penforth's face in one moment, simply so that the gentleman would stop talking!

"And as I have said, I am quite certain that her father will agree within a few moments of my asking to court her. After all, he would not have allowed me to spend so much time with his daughter if he was not pleased with me, I am sure." Looking away, Marcus gritted his jaw, fighting his desire to say something sharp in response. Again, Lord Penforth laughed derisively as a fire burned in Marcus' veins. "There must be a reason for your arrival here, however." Lord Penforth tilted his head and finally, Marcus looked back at him. "Are you simply going to stand there, sullen, or are you going to tell me what it is that you want?"

Marcus held Lord Penforth's gaze steadily, aware of the ice in the man's blue eyes. The grin on his face was a cruel one, and Marcus curled his fingers tightly into his palm, making sure to keep his voice measured.

"We are going to meet, Penforth."

He spoke without any question in his words, choosing

to state it quite plainly and distinctly - and immediately, Lord Penforth frowned.

"There is no reason for us to meet." Waving a hand dismissively, the man chuckled again, his lip now curled into something of a snarl. "Do not think that you are going to demand anything from me, Coppinger. As you may recall, *I* am the one who has a great deal of power here. If you dare say a single thing against me, if you dare try to command me, then *you* will be the one who faces consequences of the heaviest weight."

Reminding himself that Lord Penforth had no real strength, Marcus looked him straight in the eye.

"You may very well believe it to be so, but we are going to meet regardless." He kept his gaze steady and caught how Lord Penforth flinched. "Tomorrow. I will be expecting you at three in the afternoon."

"What makes you think that I shall do as you ask?" Lord Penforth sneered. "Where does this confidence come from? It is not as though you have some sort of authority here."

Snorting in derision, Lord Penforth shook his head, but Marcus did not miss the flicker in his eye – a flicker which, mayhap, spoke of concern. Bolstered, Marcus lifted his chin a notch.

"Be careful, Penforth."

Lord Penforth swiped the air between them with his hand.

"I have no intention of doing anything you ask. Your threats mean nothing."

Marcus allowed a breath of silence to grow between them before he continued, making sure to drop his voice low.

"Might I suggest that you reconsider?" Marcus tilted his head. "I am certain that you will have forgotten, but I am still very closely acquainted with Lord Fairburn. You may go and ask him to court Lady Almeria and it appears as though you fully believe and expect that the request will be granted." Marcus shrugged. "But what if I were to speak with the gentleman beforehand?"

Lord Penforth frowned.

"Then my threat of consequences still stands. I will tell all and sundry where you have been seen – starting with Lord Fairburn himself."

Marcus chuckled deep in his throat.

"Ah, but you may make a mistake there. He and I are very well acquainted, as he was the closest of friends with my father. You might think that you could simply tell him that I have been seen in a gambling den and have lost a good deal of my wealth, but you can be assured that he will not simply accept it, especially if I have spoken to him first about you. No doubt he will think you are simply being petty, saying such things only to injure me because of what I have said about you. In fact, you might have to *prove* your statement about me. Do you really wish to do such a thing? Or do you want there to be an easy escape for you at present?"

None of this was true - although Marcus had long been acquainted with Lord Fairburn, he did not have any real hope that the gentleman would give him even the smallest consideration should Lord Penforth tell him such confounded lies about Marcus' conduct. Lord Fairburn had always been very protective of his daughters, and Marcus could have no real assurance of his support. Lord Penforth did not have to know any such thing as that, however, and it was with that confidence that he allowed himself a small smile.

Lord Penforth scowled. There was not even a hint of a

smile on his face anymore, and certainly no confidence flickering about his features. His brow was deeply furrowed, his arms swinging gently by his sides as he shifted from foot to foot.

"You would not dare say anything to Lord Fairburn."

"Would I not?"

Marcus set his gaze directly at Lord Penforth, saying nothing more than that and watching how Lord Penforth's eyes flickered away from him and back again. Then he lifted his chin.

"You know what I will do."

Still, he attempts to exude confidence.

"And be that as it may, mayhap I am inclined to take the risk. I have been known, on occasion, to think of others rather than just myself – something that you cannot understand, I am sure."

With a small smile, he waited as Lord Penforth considered, only for the gentleman then to shrug and turn a little away.

"I will consider it." With only a small glance in Marcus' direction, Penforth shrugged. "And if I do decide to make my way to your townhouse, I shall not linger. I will only be a few minutes. Make sure that whatever it is you have to say can be shared in that time."

Marcus nodded, looking over his shoulder to where Lord Trevelyan stood, watching the proceedings. Giving him a small nod, he grinned in Lord Penforth's direction, though the man was already walking away.

"A few minutes will be all that I need."

The gentleman turned his head sharply, perhaps hearing the victory in Marcus' voice while his own confidence faded away. With rounded shoulders and a lowered head, he continued away from Marcus' conversation, leaving Marcus alone with his smile. Marcus' words followed his retreating back.

"That is quite satisfactory, Lord Penforth."

With a sense of triumph filling him, Marcus turned and made his way directly to Lord Trevelyan, who was looking at him somewhat quizzically.

"You have succeeded, then?"

"*More* than succeeded," Marcus chuckled, as his friend slapped him on the shoulder. "I did not give myself away, bluffed outrageously, and achieved precisely what we hoped for."

Lord Trevelyan's expression lit with a broad grin.

"Congratulations, my friend. I look forward to seeing Lord Penforth at your house tomorrow. I will be delighted to see his expression when the truth is revealed."

"As will I." Still smiling, he glanced to where Lord Penforth was still walking away, making his way determinedly to the other side of the room, as though he wished to put as must distance between Marcus and himself as possible. "He shall not have the victory. He shall not have Almeria – and that is my greatest joy."

"ARE you quite certain that he will attend?"

Confidence still brimming from yesterday's conversation with Lord Penforth, Marcus nodded.

"I am sure of it. I saw his face. He will have no other recourse *but* to attend, for after what I said about your father – which of course, was nothing more than a bluff, given that your father might *well* be disinclined towards me should he hear rumors – I saw the way his expression changed. The certainty with which I spoke gave him very little alternative but to show his face."

Smiling, he waited to see the same on Almeria's face, but it did not come. She was a good deal more nervous than he had first thought.

"You can have every assurance, Almeria." Lady Yardley smiled softly. "Lord Penforth *will* come. No doubt he will be tardy to prove that he cannot be forced into a particular course of action, but he will come here, sooner or later."

Marcus rolled his eyes.

"You should have seen how he spoke to me about you, Almeria. It was with such a brash confidence and almost an arrogance about what he would have the *moment* he spoke to your father."

His stomach rolled for a moment as a vision of Lady Almeria and Lord Penforth standing up together as husband and wife flew at him. How glad he was that such a situation would never occur!

"I shall be glad to see his face when he realizes that we know the truth." Lady Almeria's eyes flashed with a sudden anger, her brows lifting as he looked at her with gentle surprise. Seeing his look, she flushed and looked away. "No doubt you may think me a little vehement, but I confess that I will be truly glad for him to realize just how little victory he has. He has enjoyed a few weeks of power, with the belief that he is to be entirely victorious in all that he has set out to do, but in the next few minutes, he shall be forced to realize the truth – and I have no doubt that it will come as a great shock to him. However, does he not deserve such a thing? Does he not deserve to see what he has built crumble away?"

Lady Yardley nodded in evident comprehension, offering Lady Almeria a small smile.

"I can certainly see why you feel such a way, Almeria. It is *more* than understandable after what you have learned about him, and all that he has done, especially to those who care so much for you."

Her gaze traveled to Marcus, and he flushed at the knowing look she sent him. It was clear that Lady Yardley already knew precisely how Marcus felt, and mayhap was wondering why he had not yet spoken of it to Lady Almeria. Marcus opened his mouth to say something, but then closed it again, aware that now was not the time to tell her anything specific – and certainly not in company! Thankfully, Lady Almeria did not appear to notice the look shared between himself and Lady Yardley, for her gaze flicked toward the door, clearly concentrating very little on what was being said at present.

Taking a deep breath, Marcus looked towards the door also, for it was now a few minutes past three o'clock. As yet, Lord Penforth had not set foot in the door. There was a chance that he was being deliberately tardy to make sure that Marcus realized that Lord Penforth still had the power ...or, as Almeria suspected, he was not attending today at all.

"He will be seeking to exert his power." Lady Yardley smiled and spoke softly as if she could see into Marcus' mind, or hear his troublesome thoughts. "He *will* be delayed. He may be significantly so, in fact, but he will appear."

Her confidence bolstered Marcus' strength and he nodded. Taking a deep breath, he went to thank Lady Yardley, only for a tap to come at the door.

His heart leaped as he called for the butler.

"Might I bring you some refreshments, milord?"

Having been expecting Lord Penforth, Marcus' shoulders dropped as he nodded, closed his eyes, and pinched the bridge of his nose with the other hand. The butler departed swiftly, but Lady Yardley was the first to speak.

"As I have said, he will seek to maintain his power as best he can," she reminded them all. "He will arrive. All we must do is wait."

CHAPTER SEVENTEEN

*I*t was just as Lady Yardley had said.

It was nearing the next hour by the time the butler came to announce that Lord Penforth had arrived. Having almost given up hope, Marcus fought to hide his relief as he nodded to the butler, telling the man to allow Lord Penforth entry. Looking around the room he took in Lord Trevelyan's grave expression, Lady Almeria's tightly clasped hands, Lady Yardley's set gaze – and felt the same tension coil itself, like a snake, in his belly. He took a breath. The moment was now to be upon them.

"Lord Penforth."

The moment the gentleman stepped into the room, Lord Trevelyan took the same place as he had stood when Lord Wilson had entered the room. Keeping his back to the door, he made certain that Lord Penforth could not make a simple escape, and instantly Marcus saw the proud, arrogant expression on Lord Penforth's face disappear. The haughty smile faded, the sparkling eyes now narrowed as he twisted around to see exactly who was standing by the door. His gaze then settled upon Lady Almeria and, thereafter,

Lady Yardley – and upon seeing them, Lord Penforth began to splutter.

"Whatever is the meaning of this?" Throwing up his hands, he turned around, spearing Marcus with a furious gaze, but Marcus simply folded his arms across his chest, shrugged, and arched one eyebrow. Lord Penforth then swung back around towards the door, only to come to a stop as Lord Trevelyan, who was a little taller than he, and certainly broader in the shoulders, leaned back against it all the more, jutting his jaw forward as he glared at Lord Penforth. The gentleman had no other choice but to turn back. "What is this, Coppinger?" Lord Penforth twisted his head to look directly at Marcus. "You said that we needed to talk. I did not expect others to be present."

Marcus lifted one shoulder.

"I am afraid that I did not give you all of the details." He tilted his head towards Lord Trevelyan. "Surely you could have no objection to Lord Trevelyan's presence here?"

Lord Penforth snorted.

"Lord Trevelyan I can understand, but might I ask why *you* are here, Lady Almeria?" Hastily, Lord Penforth dropped his sharp tone and tried to smile as Lady Almeria lifted an eyebrow in his direction. "What I mean to say is that there is no reason for you to be here, unless you have been speaking to Lord Coppinger, who has, I am sorry to say, been telling great lies about me."

"And what lies might those be?"

Lady Almeria kept her own voice measured, though the glint in her eye lingered. Lord Penforth took a step closer to her, his hands lifted to either side, clearly ready to do whatever he could to encourage her to believe him.

"The very worst!" Lord Penforth took a small step back, his shoulders rounding. "You cannot imagine, Lady Almeria." He shot a filthy look toward Marcus. "Whatever this gentleman has been saying about me to *you*, as I am sure he has done, I can tell you that it is nothing but a falsehood."

Lady Almeria sniffed.

"Then you have *not* been threatening him?" Tipping her head, she looked first at Marcus and then slid her gaze back toward Lord Penforth. "And the fact that Lord Trevelyan has told me the same means that they must *both* be lying." She shook her head. "A most extraordinary circumstance."

"Certainly, it is."

Lord Penforth sighed and shook his head, his hands dropping to his sides as Marcus chuckled darkly.

"You are quite the accomplished liar, Penforth – and you clearly believe that Lady Almeria will trust you!" After inclining his head in Lord Trevelyan's direction, who was nodding in fervent agreement, Marcus gestured towards Lord Penforth again. "Indeed, I do not think that I have ever heard a single person lie with such fervor in an attempt to hide their guilt."

Lord Penforth sighed heavily, looking at Lady Almeria.

"You see?" he stated, as though this had been continuing for some time, throwing out one hand towards Marcus. "Can you see what I have been forced to endure? You will have been entirely unaware of it, I am sure, since so much of society is hidden from you, but it has been very trying indeed."

Marcus took a deep breath, growing tired of Lord Penforth's lies.

"Almeria. I am here to tell you the truth." He took a deep breath. "Lord Penforth did not send you those bouquets. *That* is why I was so angry with him and, after I confronted him, I followed him that particular night so that

I might speak to him clearly, reminding him that I had demanded he tell you the truth. Lord Penforth, however, chose to ignore me. Instead, he continued to state that he would pursue his attentions to you, and he thereafter attempted to blackmail me into remaining silent. I am only frustrated that I believed his threats for so long, for I see now that he has no power."

Lord Penforth's face paled, a squeak coming from his lips as he half went to say something, only for silence to follow. Lady Almeria's cheeks were pinking, her eyes fixing on Marcus as he spread out his hands.

"He did not send those flowers?"

"That is correct. Lord Penforth did not send you those bouquets, Almeria. He claimed to have done so, taking advantage of the person who had actually sent them – me. He has lied to you. He has refused to tell you the truth, despite my demands that he do so. I gave him the chance to be honorable, and he threw it back in my face."

Lady Almeria swallowed, nodded, then turned her head towards Lord Penforth, looking at him with a steady gaze. Lord Penforth himself let out an exclamation and a mutter of something unintelligible, but nothing else came from his lips.

"This is most concerning, Lord Penforth." Lady Almeria tilted her head, no astonishment in either her voice or her expression. "And to hear that Lord Coppinger attempted to offer you an opportunity for you to rectify things, but that you did not do as he suggested, is *most* displeasing. I would have thought that a gentleman would want to make certain that he was as honest and as true as he could be in his dealings with a young lady such as myself."

Lord Penforth closed his eyes, his breath shaking slightly as he let out a long breath.

"I – I am so very sorry, Lady Almeria." A cold shock immediately sent ice through his veins as Marcus stared at Lord Penforth. Was that all that was required? Marcus simply had to state the truth and Lord Penforth would, thereafter, simply capitulate and admit to it all? He had not thought the gentleman as humble as that. Lord Penforth heaved a great sigh. "The reason Lord Coppinger and Lord Trevelyan are saying such things about me is because I discovered them in a den of iniquity." He paused as Marcus let out a slow breath, realizing that he had not been wrong in his judgment of Lord Penforth. There was no real contrition here, just more lies and falsehoods in an attempt to protect himself. "I did say that I would be forced to tell society of it, unfortunately, and now it seems that I shall have to do so." Sighing heavily, Lord Penforth shook his head and spread his hands. "It is only right."

Lord Trevelyan pushed himself away from the door.

"I think you are attempting to blackmail us again." Lord Trevelyan's voice broke through the conversation and Lord Penforth shifted his gaze towards him. "That is what you said to us the night we followed you to that gambling den. The place where *you* engaged in some dark deeds."

"You may continue to speak falsehoods about me if you wish," Lord Penforth interrupted, shaking his head. "But I will not stand here and listen to this. I shall excuse myself, Lord Coppinger, and you know what will happen next."

"We did speak to Lord Wilson recently also." Marcus' words stopped Lord Penforth in his tracks. His steps, which had been turned towards the door, now came to a sudden stop, his whole body freezing in one position. Marcus smiled. "You did not think that we recognized the gentlemen in the gambling den, did you?" Lord Trevelyan chuckled, the sound flooding the room and clashing against the seriousness of the circumstances. "But I did recognize Lord Wilson, and we asked him to call. You can imagine our astonishment when he told us the truth, which was that he knew none of what you had said to either myself or Lord Coppinger. He also told us that the reason you were there was to make payment for a debt – a great and heavy debt, I might add, and one which I am certain is not alone in its weight." Lord Penforth clenched his hands into tight fists, his jaw tensed as he stood, straight-backed and eyes blazing. "After talking to the gentleman, we knew that we no longer had to fear the supposed consequences you would bring upon us. There was nothing you could do or say which would make any difference to our lives. Should you begin to spread rumors about us, the only thing which would occur would be damage to your own reputation, given that both Lord Trevelyan and I are gentlemen of the *ton* in excellent standing."

This was said without any sense of arrogance, but rather clearly and quite plainly. Marcus kept his gaze steadily upon Lord Penforth, whose eyes were so tightly squeezed shut, there were lines drawn between his eyes and his temples. His hands were tight fists, his shoulders lifted, his whole frame tight with an obvious and furious anger – but was it anger directed towards Marcus or was it simply because he had been found out?

"You surely cannot believe a word of this, Lady Almeria."

Lord Penforth's voice was low, hissing between his thin lips, but Lady Almeria only laughed.

"Good gracious Lord Penforth, you cannot truly imagine that I would believe the word of a gentleman I have known only a few weeks over that of the gentleman I have known my entire life?" Lord Penforth opened his eyes and looked at her. She waved one hand in his direction, as though shooing him away. "Truly, you are a foolish sort. I am glad to be free of you."

"Foolish?" Lord Penforth practically screeched. "My dear lady, only a few minutes ago you would have thought me the very best gentleman in London! Now, after speaking with Lord Coppinger, you state that I am the very worst! How can such a thing be? You do me an unfairness."

Lady Almeria turned her head towards Lord Penforth and, after a moment, she rose to her feet.

"Understand this, Lord Penforth." She spoke slowly, as she did not want him to miss a single word, her chin lifted, her gaze steady. "I do not think you the very best of gentlemen, nor do I think you an excellent gentleman. You told me that you sent me bouquets, but I now discover that you have lied to me about it – but before I even knew that, I was set against you. Your arrogance, your mockery of others, your lack of interest in anything which I have to say, as well as your continual disregard for my feelings and the feelings of others – none of your characteristics are traits that I find in the least bit delightful. I am afraid, Lord Penforth, that I was eager to remove myself from you. How glad I am, now that Lord Coppinger and Lord Trevelyan have made it so easy for me to do so. You and I will no longer be in company together. You will *not* be speaking to my father, and certainly, I will never allow myself to be courted by you. To hear that you have done as much as you can to threaten my dear friend, and Lord Trevelyan with him, simply so that you might attempt to gain my hand, is beyond despicable."

"But I need you!" With a sudden ferocity, Lord Penforth flung himself towards Lady Almeria, his hand grabbing her arm, attempting to pull her to himself. "I need you, Lady Almeria. I have debts and only you–"

"Unhand her at once!" Marcus rushed forward, grasping Lord Penforth bodily, breaking his grasp on Almeria's arm, and then dragging him towards the door. "You will make your way from this house, and you will never come near Lady Almeria again. You will not so much as breathe a word against either myself or Lord Trevelyan – or indeed, ever threaten another person again." Lord Trevelyan opened the door wide for them both and Marcus shoved Lord Penforth through it, leaving him gasping for air, his eyes wide as he stared at them both. "And I am afraid that all of society will know exactly who you are, and of your many debts, as you yourself have stated," Marcus finished, breathing hard. "Now leave my house! Your power is gone, your petty attempt at victory is broken, and you shall be the one to shoulder the consequences."

Lord Penforth glared at them both, standing framed in the doorway, seemingly reluctant to leave, even though his entire cruelty had been laid out for all of them to see.

"Not everyone will believe you," he hissed, a hint of a smile on his face. "It will be your word against my own."

"You are aware that Lady Yardley has been sitting here with us?" Lord Trevelyan gestured to the lady and Lord Penforth's face immediately went white. "She is well known and well respected, and her publication, 'The London Ledger' is known to always be truthful. Lady Yardley is most careful about what is printed within the Ledger, and I am delighted to say that this afternoon's conversation will go within it. Then society will know that you are a man who often frequents gambling dens, has a great many debts, and who sought only to marry Lady Almeria for her wealth whilst pretending to care for her."

Lord Penforth's mouth opened and closed like that of a fish, but he could not say anything more – and much to

Marcus' delight, the butler appeared. With a grin, Marcus gestured towards Lord Penforth.

"Lord Penforth was just about to remove himself from my house. He is not to be welcomed back into my presence at *any* time," Marcus directed firmly, feeling such a great sense of relief that the matter was now at an end, that he could not help but chuckle at Lord Penforth's stupefied expression. "Good afternoon, Lord Penforth. I am glad to say that we will never be in company again."

So saying, he turned on his heel and he and Lord Trevelyan walked back into the drawing room, with Marcus closing the door firmly behind him. He immediately found himself laughing, overwhelmed with all that he felt, and within minutes the whole room rang with peals of mirth. There was relief in everyone's expression and Marcus' heart swelled all the more at the delight in Lady Almeria's expression.

"I do hope I did not overstate things." Lord Trevelyan tipped his head towards Lady Yardley. "You will write about this matter in 'The London Ledger', I hope?"

Lady Yardley chuckled.

"My dear Lord Trevelyan, of course I shall. I pride myself on writing nothing but truth in the Ledger and I will be *more* than delighted to reveal this to all of those who read my little publication. Whether he wishes it or not, Lord Penforth's dark deeds will finally be exposed to all, and he will no longer be able to continue in such a way, not with anyone."

"I would be surprised if he remained in society once the truth comes out." Lord Trevelyan walked across to the room to pour brandy, but Marcus turned to Lady Almeria, seeing how she looked at him. She was sitting down again, but looking up at him with eyes that were brimming with obviously happy tears, her lips curved in a beautiful smile. Marcus' heart lurched. He had something more to say to her, something all the more important, but for the moment, it had to remain hidden behind his lips, clasped tightly against his heart. Their time would come very soon, a time when he would be able to tell her everything and pray that she felt even the smallest modicum of affection in return. "To our victory."

Handing a brandy to Marcus, Lord Trevelyan then gave one to Lady Yardley and a small glass to Lady Almeria, who accepted it somewhat gingerly. Then he lifted his glass and Marcus clinked it lightly with his own.

"To our victory," Marcus repeated as he looked across at Lady Almeria, hoping their future would be just as bright as this moment.

EPILOGUE

"*A*lmeria."

The moment Marcus stepped into the room, Almeria's heart quickened into a flurry. She remained precisely where she was, her legs all a tremble, and thus she did not stand.

"Marcus, come in. Lady Yardley and Lady Sherbourne are just gone to..."

She did not know where they had gone but she was glad of their absence, especially when her eyes were full of Marcus. There was something unspoken and yet fully declared between them, something she knew would be the fulfillment of all of her hopes. How strange this Season had been, and yet how wonderful all at the same time. She was sure that Marcus was about to offer her more than she had ever expected, and she was ready to grasp it with both hands.

"You have seen 'The London Ledger', I assume?" A quick grin flashed across his face as she nodded. "I do not think that Lord Penforth will be much in society from now on."

"I would highly doubt it."

Her heart began to beat a little more quickly and she rose from her seat, as though it were urging her forward into the next part of the conversation.

"I must say, Lady Yardley did very well. She was tactful but clear."

Marcus smiled at her and Almeria's hand reached out, instinctively, grasping his own as he came a little closer to her, so that they stood together in the middle of the room.

"I am sure that all of the young women of the *ton* will be careful not to go anywhere near him." Did he feel the slight tremble that ran through her at his touch? Taking a deep breath, she tilted her head to one side, wishing now for him to talk about something *other* than Lord Penforth. "You are quite satisfied too, I hope?"

"Satisfied?" Lord Coppinger inclined his head, no smile on his face, but a gentleness about his eyes which sent a fresh flurry of warmth scurrying through her veins. "No, Almeria, I would not say that I am satisfied."

Her response was swallowed away by the rising tide of emotion, her heart seeming to come to a stop as his fingers shifted, seeking to lace through her own, his dark grey eyes swirling like clouds before they parted to reveal the horizon. Her stomach was turning this way and that, and yet such happiness was beginning to fill her whole being, it was as though she could not quite breathe for the joy of it.

"I have something to tell you, Almeria," Lord Coppinger continued, his chest rising and falling steadily but his voice low. "No doubt you will either think me a fool for having waited so long, or be utterly astonished at what I have to say, but I cannot hide the truth from you any longer." Taking another breath, he found her other hand, then smiled. "Almeria, I have loved you for almost as long as I have had breath."

Such was the beauty of the moment, Almeria could do nothing but take it into herself, wrapping it tightly around her heart as she let her lips curve into a smile of utter happiness. There was no astonishment, no great sweep of gasping delight but rather a joy that rang through her, offering her a sweetness that she had never before tasted.

"Oh, Marcus."

Moving closer to him still, she laughed softly at the way his eyes widened, as though he were still waiting for her to say something more, something which would tell him what his future was to be. Pulling her fingers from his, she cupped his face in gentle hands, smiling up at him and seeing his eyes close for a moment as he let out a breath of relief.

"You mean to say there might be some hope for my future with you?"

"More than a hope, my dear Marcus." Tilting her head, Almeria laughed again softly at his reaction. "Much more than a hope."

His hands pressed to hers.

"I assume then, that you knew already that I was the one who had sent you those flowers? You did not appear surprised at my initial confession, although I had been uncertain as to why that might be."

She brushed her thumb across his cheek as he dropped his hands to her waist.

"Yes, Marcus, although I confess that it was not I who first understood it. It was Miss Madeley! I believe she was suspicious for some time, long before I had any idea of your affection."

Marcus finally smiled, his hands tight around her waist

now, encouraging her forward so that they stood closer than they had ever been.

"What was it that gave me away?"

"I believe it was the fact that you asked Lord Penforth which two flowers were in my bouquet. She then asked me whether or not I had ever informed you that there were only two flowers within my most recent bouquet, and I had to admit that I did not think I had."

Throwing his head back, Marcus let out a low groan.

"That was a mistake on my part, but might I ask..." Lowering his gaze again, he lifted one hand and ran soft fingers lightly down her cheek, making her heart pound furiously. "Might I ask if you had any uncertainty as to what you felt at that moment?"

Seeing his concern, she shook her head.

"I confess that I found it more of a relief." Again, she laughed when his eyes cleared. "It was a relief to know that I was not alone in my feelings. I had been battling strange feelings and emotions deep within myself, uncertain of what I felt, and why I was pulled towards you in such a way! You cannot know how glad I was to understand it all, to see that the person I had always been drawn to, the person who I had always loved, was none other than you."

Lord Coppinger swallowed hard, seeming unable to speak for a moment as his hands once more pulled her tight against him.

"My dear Almeria."

His voice rasped as he lowered his head and, without hesitation, kissed her.

Almeria had often wondered what it would feel like to be kissed by a gentleman, but she had never expected a great fire of feeling to envelop her so. Marcus' lips were soft, yet encouraging, almost urging her to respond and, after a moment, she did as he bade her. Her hands crept up around his shoulders, going tight around his neck as his arms held her gently around her waist. How long the kiss lasted, Almeria could not say, for it felt as though it were a breath and yet a lifetime, all in one moment. It was the fulfillment of hopes she had never known she'd held, and now, her future was secure with this man who held her so carefully.

She loved him. She loved this gentleman who had long called himself her friend and now had become all the more to her. How much she cared for him, how much she adored him! She could not bring herself to separate from him again.

With a sudden gasp, she broke the kiss, looking into his eyes. Marcus blinked, looking at her, his face rather flushed as his eyes searched her face.

"We *are* going to marry, are we not?"

Instantly his face split with a smile as he chuckled, making Almeria's fears ebb away in an instant.

"Of course, we shall," he promised, bending down to brush her lips with his again for just a moment. "We shall be husband and wife, just as soon as I can arrange it." Gentle fingers pushed back a tendril of hair behind her ear, as he smiled down into her eyes. There was so much love evident there, Almeria wondered why she had not recognized it long before, why it had taken her so much time to see what – and who – was standing in her heart from the very beginning.

"I love you, Almeria."

She smiled and lifted her lips to his once more.

"And I love you."

I AM glad Marcus and Almeria finally realized they love each other! I love a childhood sweetheart story!

190 | ROSE PEARSON

Don't miss the next one in the Only for Love series! The Viscount's Unlikely Ally

Did you miss the first book in the **Only for Love** series? The Heart of a Gentleman Read ahead for a sneak peek!

READ THIS ONE? Try one of my favorites! Convenient Arrangements: A Regency Romance Collection

MY DEAR READER

Thank you for reading and supporting my books! I hope this story brought you some escape from the real world into the always captivating Regency world. A good story, especially one with a happy ending, just brightens your day and makes you feel good! If you enjoyed the book, would you leave a review on Amazon? Reviews are always appreciated.

Below is a complete list of all my books! Why not click and see if one of them can keep you entertained for a few hours?

The Duke's Daughters Series
The Duke's Daughters: A Sweet Regency Romance Boxset
A Rogue for a Lady
My Restless Earl
Rescued by an Earl
In the Arms of an Earl
The Reluctant Marquess (Prequel)

A Smithfield Market Regency Romance
The Smithfield Market Romances: A Sweet Regency
Romance Boxset
The Rogue's Flower
Saved by the Scoundrel
Mending the Duke
The Baron's Malady

The Returned Lords of Grosvenor Square
The Returned Lords of Grosvenor Square: A Regency
Romance Boxset
The Waiting Bride
The Long Return
The Duke's Saving Grace
A New Home for the Duke

The Spinsters Guild
The Spinsters Guild: A Sweet Regency Romance Boxset
A New Beginning
The Disgraced Bride
A Gentleman's Revenge
A Foolish Wager
A Lord Undone

Convenient Arrangements
Convenient Arrangements: A Regency Romance
Collection
A Broken Betrothal
In Search of Love
Wed in Disgrace
Betrayal and Lies
A Past to Forget
Engaged to a Friend

Landon House
Landon House: A Regency Romance Boxset
Mistaken for a Rake
A Selfish Heart
A Love Unbroken
A Christmas Match
A Most Suitable Bride

An Expectation of Love

Second Chance Regency Romance
Second Chance Regency Romance Boxset
Loving the Scarred Soldier
Second Chance for Love
A Family of her Own
A Spinster No More

Soldiers and Sweethearts
To Trust a Viscount
Whispers of the Heart
Dare to Love a Marquess
Healing the Earl
A Lady's Brave Heart

Ladies on their Own: Governesses and Companions
Ladies on their Own Boxset
More Than a Companion
The Hidden Governess
The Companion and the Earl
More than a Governess
Protected by the Companion

Lost Fortunes, Found Love
A Viscount's Stolen Fortune
For Richer, For Poorer
Her Heart's Choice
A Dreadful Secret
Their Forgotten Love
His Convenient Match

Only for Love

The Heart of a Gentleman
A Lord or a Liar
The Earl's Unspoken Love
The Viscount's Unlikely Ally

Christmas Stories
Love and Christmas Wishes: Three Regency Romance
Novellas
A Family for Christmas
Mistletoe Magic: A Regency Romance
Heart, Homes & Holidays: A Sweet Romance Anthology

Happy Reading!
All my love,
Rose

A SNEAK PEEK OF THE
HEART OF A GENTLEMAN

CHAPTER ONE

"*T*hank you again for sponsoring me through this Season." Lady Cassandra Chilton pressed her hands together tightly, a delighted smile spreading across her features as excitement quickened her heart. Having spent a few years in London, with the rest of her family, it was now finally her turn to come out into society. "I would not have been able to come to London had you not been so generous."

Norah, Lady Yardley smiled softly and slipped her arm through Cassandra's.

"I am just as glad as you to have you here, cousin." A small sigh slipped from her, and her expression was gentle. "It does not seem so long ago that I was here myself, to make my Come Out."

Cassandra's happiness faded just a little

"Your first marriage was not of great length, I recall." Pressing her lips together immediately, she winced, dropping her head, hugely embarrassed by her own forthrightness "Forgive me. I ought not to be speaking of such things."

Thankfully, Lady Yardley chuckled.

198 | ROSE PEARSON

"You need not be so concerned, my dear. You are right to say that my first marriage was not of long duration, but I *have* found a great happiness since then - more than that, in fact. I have found a love which has brought me such wondrous contentment that I do not think I should ever have been able to live without it." At this, Cassandra found herself sighing softly, her eyes roving around the London streets as though they might land on the very gentleman who would thereafter bring her the same love, within her own heart, that her cousin spoke of. "But you must be cautious," her cousin continued. "There are many gentlemen in London – even more during the Season – and not *all* of them will seek the same sort of love match as you. Therefore, you must always be cautious, my dear."

A little surprised at this, Cassandra looked at her cousin as they walked along the London streets.

"I must be cautious?"

Her cousin nodded sagely.

"Yes, most careful, my dear. Society is not always as it appears. It can be a fickle friend." Lady Yardley glanced at Cassandra then quickly smiled - a smile which Cassandra did not immediately believe. "Pray, do not allow me to concern you, not when you have only just arrived in London!" She shook her head and let out an exasperated sigh, evidently directed towards herself. "No doubt you will have a wonderful Season. With so much to see and to enjoy, I am certain that these months will be delightful."

Cassandra allowed herself a small smile, her shoulders relaxing in gentle relief. She had always assumed that London society would be warm and welcoming and, whilst there was always the danger of scandal, that danger came only from young ladies or gentlemen choosing to behave improperly. Given that she was quite determined *not* to behave so, there could be no danger of scandal for her!

"I assure you, Norah, that I shall be impeccable in my behavior and in my speech. You need not concern yourself over that."

Lady Yardley touched her hand for a moment.

"I am sure that you shall. I have never once considered otherwise." She offered a quick smile. "But you will also learn a great deal about society and the gentlemen within it – and that will stand you in good stead."

Still not entirely certain, and pondering what her cousin meant, Cassandra found her thoughts turned in an entirely new direction when she saw someone she recognized. Miss Bridget Wynch was accompanied by another young lady who Cassandra knew, and with a slight squeal of excitement, she made to rush towards them – somehow managing to drag Lady Yardley with her. When Cassandra turned to apologize, her cousin laughingly disentangled herself and then urged Cassandra to continue to her friends. Cassandra did so without hesitation and, despite the fact it was in the middle of London, the three young ladies embraced each other openly, their voices high with excitement. Over the last few years, they had come to know each other as they had accompanied various elder siblings to London, alongside their parents. Now it was to be their turn and the joy of that made Cassandra's heart sing.

"You are here then, Cassandra." Lady Almeria grasped her hand tightly. "And you were so concerned that your father would not permit you to come."

"It was not that he was unwilling to permit me to attend, rather that he was concerned that he would be on the continent at the time," Cassandra explained. "In that regard, he was correct, for both my father *and* my mother have taken leave of England, and have gone to my father's properties on the continent. I am here, however, and stay now with my cousin." Turning, she gestured to Lady Yardley who was standing only a short distance away, a warm smile on her face. She did not move forward, as though she was unwilling to interrupt the conversation and, with a smile of gratitude, Cassandra turned back to her friends. "We are to make our first appearances in Society tomorrow." Stating this, she let out a slow breath. "How do you each feel?"

With a slight squeal, Miss Wynch closed her eyes and shuddered.

"Yes, we are, and I confess that I am quite terrified." Taking a breath, she pressed one hand to her heart. "I am very afraid that I will make a fool of myself in some way."

"As am I," Lady Almeria agreed. "I am afraid that I shall trip over my gown and fall face first in front of the most important people of the *ton*! Then what shall be said of me?"

"They will say that you may not be the most elegant young lady to dance with?" Cassandra suggested, as her friends giggled. "However, I am quite sure that you will have a great deal of poise – as you always do – and will be able to control your nerves quite easily. You will not so much as stumble."

"I thank you for your faith in me."

Lady Almeria let out a slow breath.

"Our other friends will be present also," Miss Wynch added. "How good it will be to see them again – both at our presentation and at the ball in the evening!"

Cassandra smiled at the thought of the ball, her stomach twisting gently with a touch of nervousness.

"I admit to being excited about our first ball also. I do

wonder which gentlemen we shall dance with." Lady Almeria swiveled her head around, looking at the many passersby before leaning forward a little more and dropping her voice low. "I am hopeful that one or two may become of significant interest to us."

Cassandra's smile fell.

"My cousin has warned me to be cautious when it comes to the gentlemen of London." Still a little disconcerted by what Lady Yardley had said to her, Cassandra gave her friends a small shrug. "I do not understand precisely what she meant, but there is something about the gentlemen of London of which we must be careful. My cousin has not explained to me precisely what that is as yet, but states that there is much I must learn. I confess to you, since we have all been in London before, for previous Seasons – albeit not for ourselves – I did not think that there would be a great deal for me to understand."

"I do not know what things Lady Yardley speaks of," Miss Wynch agreed, a small frown between her eyebrows now. "My elder sister did not have any difficulty with *her* husband. When they met, they were so delighted with each other they were wed within six weeks."

"I confess I know very little about Catherine's engagement and marriage," Lady Almeria replied, speaking of her elder sister who was some ten years her senior. "But I *do* know that Amanda had a little trouble, although I believe that came from the realization that she had to choose which gentleman was to be her suitor. She had *three* gentlemen eager to court her – all deserving gentlemen too – and therefore, she had some trouble in deciding who was best suited."

Cassandra frowned, her nose wrinkling.

"I could not say anything about my brother's marriage, but my sister did wait until her second Season before she accepted a gentleman's offer of courtship. She spoke very little to me of any difficulties, however - and therefore, I do not understand what my cousin means." A small sigh escaped her. "I do wish that my sister and I had been a little closer. She might have spoken to me of whatever difficulties she faced, whether they were large or small, but in truth, she said very little to me. Had she done so, then I might be already aware of whatever it is that Lady Yardley wishes to convey."

Miss Wynch put one hand on her arm.

"I am sure that we shall find out soon enough." She shrugged. "I do not think that you need to worry about it either, given that we have more than enough to think about! Maybe after our come out, Lady Yardley will tell you all."

Cassandra took a deep breath and let herself smile as the tension flooded out of her.

"Yes, you are right." Throwing a quick glance back towards her cousin, who was still standing nearby, she spread both hands. "Regardless of what is said, I am still determined to marry for love."

"As am I." Lady Almeria's lips tipped into a soft smile. "In fact, I think that all of us – our absent friends included – are determined to marry for love. Did we not all say so last Season, as we watched our sisters and brothers make their matches? I find myself just as resolved today as I was then. I do not think our desires a foolish endeavor."

Cassandra shook her head.

"Nor do I, although my brother would have a different opinion, given that he trumpeted how excellent a match he made with his new bride."

With a wry laugh, she tilted her head, and looked from one friend to the other.

"And my sister would have laughed at us for such a

suggestion, I confess," Lady Almeria agreed. "She states practicality to be the very best of situations, but I confess I dream of more."

"As do I." A slightly wistful expression came over Miss Wynch as she clasped both hands to her heart, her eyes closing for a moment. "I wish to know that a gentleman's heart is filled only with myself, rather than looking at me as though I am some acquisition suitable for his household."

Such a description made Cassandra shudder as she nodded fervently. To be chosen by a gentleman simply due to her father's title, or for her dowry, would be most displeasing. To Cassandra's mind, it would not bring any great happiness.

"Then I have a proposal." Cassandra held out her hands, one to each of her friends. "What say you we promise each other – here and now, that we shall *only* marry for love and shall support each other in our promises to do so? We can speak to our other friends and seek their agreement also."

Catching her breath, Lady Almeria nodded fervently, her smile spreading across her face.

"It sounds like a wonderful idea."

"I quite agree." Miss Wynch smiled back at her, reaching to grasp Cassandra's hand. "We shall speak to the others soon, I presume?"

"Yes, of course. We shall have a merry little band together and, in time, we are certain to have success." Cassandra sighed contentedly, the last flurries of tension going from her. "We will all find ourselves suitable matches with gentlemen to whom we can lose our hearts, knowing that their hearts love us in return."

As her friends smiled, Cassandra's heart began to soar. This Season was going to be an excellent one, she was sure.

Yes, she had her cousin's warnings, but she also had her friends' support in her quest to find a gentleman who would love her; a gentleman she would carry in her heart for all of her days. Surely such a fellow would not be so difficult to find?

CHAPTER TWO

"*I* should like to hear something... significant... about you this Season."

Jonathan rolled his eyes, knowing precisely what his mother expected. This was now his fourth Season in London and, as yet, he had not found himself a bride – much to his mother's chagrin, of course. On his part, it was quite deliberate and, although he had stated as much to his mother on various occasions, it did not seem to alter her attempts to encourage him toward matrimony.

"You are aware that you did not have to come to London with me, Mother?" Jonathan shrugged his shoulders. "If you had remained at home, then you would not have suffered as much concern, surely?"

"It is a legitimate concern, which I would suffer equally, no matter where I am!" his mother shot back fiercely. "You have not given me any expectation of a forthcoming marriage and I continually wonder and worry over the lack of an heir! You are the Marquess of Sherbourne! You have responsibilities!"

Jonathan scowled.

"Responsibilities I take seriously, Mother. However, I will not be forced into–"

"I have already heard whispers of your various entanglements during last Season. I can hardly imagine that this Season will be any better."

At this, Jonathan took a moment to gather himself, trying to control the fierce surge of anger now burning in his soul. When he spoke, it was with a quietness he could barely keep hold of.

"I assure you, such whispers have been greatly exaggerated. I am not a scoundrel."

He could tell immediately that this did not please his mother, for she shook her head and let out a harsh laugh.

"I do not believe that," she stated, her tone still fierce. "Especially when my *dear* friend, Lady Edmonds, tells me that you were attempting to entice her daughter into your arms!" Her eyes closed tight. "The fact that she is still willing to even be my friend is very generous indeed."

A slight pang of guilt edged into Jonathan's heart, but he ignored it with an easy shrug of his shoulders.

"Do you truly think that Lady Hannah was so unwilling? That I had to coerce her somehow?" Seeing how his mother pressed one hand to her mouth, he rolled his eyes for the second time. "It is the truth I tell you, Mother. Whether you wish to believe me or not, any rumors you have heard have been greatly exaggerated. For example, Lady Hannah was the one who came to seek *me* out, rather than it being me pursuing her."

His mother rose from her chair, her chin lifting and her face a little flushed.

"I will not believe that Lady Hannah, who is so delicate a creature, would even have *dreamt* of doing such a thing as that!"

"You very may very well not believe it, and that would not surprise me, given that everyone else holds much the same opinion." Spreading both hands, Jonathan let out a small sigh. "I may not be eager to wed, Mother, but I certainly am not a scoundrel or a rogue, as you appear to believe me to be."

His mother looked away, her hands planted on her hips, and Jonathan scowled, frustrated by his mother's lack of belief in his character. During last Season, he had been utterly astonished when Lady Hannah had come to speak with him directly, only to attempt to draw him into some sort of assignation. And she only in her first year out in Society as well! Jonathan had always kept far from those young ladies who were newly out – even, as in this case, from those who had been so very obvious in their eagerness. No doubt being a little upset by his lack of willingness, Lady Hannah had gone on to tell her mother a deliberate untruth about him, suggesting that *he* had been the one to try to negotiate something warm between them. And now, it seemed, his own mother believed that same thing. It was not the first time that such rumors had been spread about gentlemen – himself included and, on some occasions, Jonathan admitted, the rumors had come about because of his actions. But other whispers, such as this, were grossly unfair. Yet who would believe the word of a supposedly roguish gentleman over that of a young lady? There was, Jonathan considered, very little point in arguing.

"I will not go near Lady Hannah this Season, if that is what is concerning you." With a slight lift of his shoulders, Jonathan tried to smile at his mother, but only received an angry glare in return. "I assure you that I have no interest in Lady Hannah! She is not someone I would consider even stepping out with, were I given the opportunity." Protesting his innocence was futile, he knew, but yet the words kept coming. "I do not even think her overly handsome."

"Are you stating that she is ugly?"

Jonathan closed his eyes, stifling a groan. It seemed that he could say nothing which would bring his mother any satisfaction. The only thing to please her would be if he declared himself betrothed to a suitable young lady. At present, however, he had very little intention of doing anything of the sort. He was quite content with his life, such as it was. The time to continue the family line would come soon enough, but he could give it a few more years until he had to consider it.

"No, mother, Lady Hannah is not ugly." Seeing how her frown lifted just a little, he took his opportunity to escape. "Now, if you would excuse me, I have an afternoon tea to attend." His mother's eyebrows lifted with evident hope, but Jonathan immediately set her straight. "With Lord and Lady Yardley," he added, aware of how quickly her features slumped again. "I have no doubt that you will be a little frustrated by the fact that my ongoing friendship with Lord and Lady Yardley appears to be the most significant connection in my life, but he is a dear friend and his wife has become so also. Surely you can find no complaint there!" His mother sniffed and looked away, and Jonathan, believing now that there was very little he could say to even bring a smile to his mother's face, turned his steps towards the door. "Good afternoon, Mother."

So saying, he strode from the room, fully aware of the heavy weight of expectation that his mother continually placed upon his shoulders. He could not give her what she wanted, and her ongoing criticism was difficult to hear. She did not have proof of his connection to Lady Hannah but, all the same, thought poorly of him. She would criticize his close acquaintance with Lord and Lady Yardley also! His friendships were quickly thrown aside, as were his explanations and his pleadings of innocence - there was nothing he could say or do that would bring her even a hint of satisfaction, and Jonathan had no doubt that, during this Season, he would be a disappointment to her all over again.

"Good afternoon, Yardley."

His friend beamed at him, turning his head for a moment as he poured two measures of brandy into two separate glasses.

"Sherbourne! Good afternoon, do come in. It appears to be an excellent afternoon, does it not?"

Jonathan did so, his eyes on his friend, gesturing to the brandy on the table.

"It will more than excellent once you hand me the glass which I hope is mine."

Lord Yardley chuckled and obliged him.

"And yet, it seems as though you are troubled all the same," he remarked, as Jonathan took a sip of what he knew to be an excellent French brandy. "Come then, what troubles you this time?" Lifting an eyebrow, he grinned as Jonathan groaned aloud. "I am certain it will have something to do with your dear mother."

Letting out an exasperated breath, Jonathan gesticulated in the air as Lord Yardley took a seat opposite him.

"She wishes me to be just as you are." Jonathan took a small sip of his brandy. "Whereas I am less and less inclined to wed myself to *any* young lady who has her approval... simply because she will have my mother's approval!"

Lord Yardley chuckled and then took a sip from his

glass.

"That is difficult indeed! You are quite right to state that *you* will be the one to decide when you wed... so long as it is not simply because you are avoiding your responsibilities."

"I am keenly aware of my responsibilities, which is precisely *why* I avoid matrimony. I already have a great deal of demands on my time – I can only imagine that to add a wife to that burden would only increase it!"

"You are quite mistaken."

Jonathan chuckled darkly.

"You only say so because your wife is an exceptional lady. I think you one of the *few* gentlemen who finds themselves so blessed."

Lord Yardley shrugged.

"Then I must wonder if you believe the state of matrimony to be a death knell to a gentleman's heart. I can assure you it is quite the opposite."

"You say that only because you have found contentment," Jonathan shot back quickly. "There are many gentlemen who do not find themselves so comfortable."

Lord Yardley shrugged.

"There may be more than you know." He picked up his brandy glass again. "And if that is what you seek from your forthcoming marriage to whichever young lady you choose, then why do you not simply search for a suitable match, rather than doing very little other than entertain yourself throughout the Season? You could find a lady who would bring you a great deal of contentment, I am sure."

Resisting the urge to roll his eyes, Jonathan spread both hands, one still clutching his brandy, the other one empty.

"Because I do not feel the same urgency about the matter as my mother," he stated firmly. "When the time is right, I will find an excellent young lady who will fill my heart with such great affection that I will be unable to do anything but look into her eyes and find myself lost. *Then* I will know that she is the one I ought to wed. However, until that moment comes, I will continue on, just as I am at present." For a moment he thought that his friend would laugh at him, but much to his surprise, Lord Yardley simply nodded in agreement. There was not even a hint of a smile on his lips, but rather a gentle understanding in his eyes which spoke of acceptance of all that Jonathan had said. "Let us talk of something other than my present situation." Throwing back the rest of his brandy, and with a great and contented sigh, Jonathan set the glass back down on the table to his right. "Your other guests have not arrived as yet, I see. Are you hoping for a jovial afternoon?"

"A cheerful afternoon, certainly, although we will not be overwhelmed by too many guests today." Lord Yardley grinned. "It is a little unfortunate that I shall soon have to return to my estate." His smile faded a little. "I do not like the idea of being away from my wife, but there are many improvements taking place at the estate which must be over-seen." His lips pulled to one side for a moment. "Besides which, my wife has her cousin to chaperone this Season."

"Her cousin?" Repeating this, Jonathan frowned as his friend nodded. "You did not mention this to me before."

"Did I not?" Lord Yardley replied mildly, waving one hand as though it did not matter. "Yes, my wife is to be chaperoning her cousin for the duration of the Season. The girl's parents are both on the continent, you understand, and given that she would not have much of a coming out otherwise, my wife thought it best to offer."

Jonathan tried to ignore the frustration within him at the fact that his friend would not be present for the Season, choosing instead to nod.

"How very kind of her. And what is the name of this cousin?"

"Lady Cassandra Chilton." Lord Yardley's gaze flew towards the door. "No doubt you will meet her this afternoon. I do not know what is taking them so long but, then again, I have never been a young lady about to make her first appearance in Society."

Jonathan blinked. Clearly this was more than just an afternoon tea. This Lady Cassandra would be present this afternoon so that she might become acquainted with a few of those within society. Why Lord Yardley had not told him about this before, Jonathan did not know – although it was very like his friend to forget about such details.

"Lady Cassandra is being presented this afternoon?"

His friend nodded.

"Yes, as we speak. I did offer to go with them, of course, but was informed she was already nervous enough, and would be quite contented with just my dear wife standing beside her."

Jonathan nodded and was about to make some remark about how difficult a moment it must be for a young lady to be presented to the Queen, only for the door to open and Lady Yardley herself to step inside.

"Ah, Lord Sherbourne. How delighted I am to see you."

With a genuine smile on her face, she waved at him to remain seated rather than attempt to get up to greet her.

"Good afternoon, Lady Yardley. I do hope the presentation went well?"

"Exceptionally well. Cassandra has just gone up to change out of her presentation gown – those gowns which the Queen requires are so outdated and uncomfortable! She will join us shortly."

The lady threw a broad smile in the direction of her

husband, who then rose immediately from his chair to go towards her. Taking her hands, he pressed a kiss to the back of one and then to the back of the other. It was a display of affection usually reserved only for private moments, but Jonathan was well used to such things between Lord and Lady Yardley. In many ways, he found it rather endearing.

"I am sure that Cassandra did very well with you beside her."

Lady Yardley smiled at her husband.

"She has a great deal of strength," she replied, quietly. "I find her quite remarkable. Indeed, I was proud to be there beside her."

"I have only just been hearing about your cousin, Lady Yardley. I do hope to be introduced to her very soon." Shifting in his chair, Jonathan waved his empty glass at Lord Yardley, who laughed but went in search of the brandy regardless. "You are sponsoring her through the Season, I understand."

His gaze now fixed itself on Lady Yardley, aware of that soft smile on her face.

"Yes, I am." Settling herself in her chair, she let out a small sigh as she did so. "I have no doubt that she will be a delight to society. She is young and beautiful and very well-considered, albeit a little naïve."

A slight frown caught Jonathan's forehead.

"Naïve?"

Lady Yardley nodded.

"Yes, just as every young lady new to society has been, and will be for years to come. She is quite certain that she will find herself hopelessly in love with the very best of a gentleman and that he will seek to marry her by the end of the Season."

"Such things do happen, my dear."

Lady Yardley laughed softly at Lord Yardley's remark, reaching across from her chair to grasp her husband's hand.

"I am not saying that they do not, only that my dear cousin thinks that all will be marvelously well for her in society and that the *ton* is a welcoming creature rather than one to be most cautious of. I, however, am much more on my guard. Not every gentleman who seeks her out will be looking to marry her. Not every gentleman who seeks her out will believe in the concept of love."

"Love?" Jonathan snorted, rolling his eyes to himself as both Lord and Lady Yardley turned their attention towards him. Flushing, he shrugged. "I suppose I would count myself as someone who does not believe such a thing to have any importance. I may not even believe in the concept!"

Lady Yardley's eyes opened wide.

"You mean to say that what Lord Yardley and I share is something you do not believe in?"

Blinking rapidly, Jonathan tried to explain, his chest suddenly tight.

"No, it is not that I do not believe it a meaningful connection which can be found between two people such as yourselves. It is that I personally have no interest in it. I have no intention of marrying someone simply because I find myself in love with them. In truth, I do not know if I am even capable of such a feeling."

"I can assure you that you are, whether or not you believe yourself to be."

Lord Yardley muttered his remark rather quietly and Jonathan took in a slow breath, praying that his friend would not start instructing him on the matter of love."

Lady Yardley smiled and gazed at Jonathan for some moments before taking a breath and continuing.

"All the same, I do want my cousin to be cautious, particularly during this evening's ball. I want her to understand that not every gentleman will be as she expects."

"I am sure such gentlemen will make that obvious all by themselves."

This brought a frown to Lady Yardley's features, but a chuckle came from Lord Yardley instead. Jonathan grinned, just as the door opened and a young lady stepped into the room, beckoned by Lady Yardley. A gentle smile softened her delicate features as she glanced around the room, her eyes finally lingering on Jonathan.

"I feel as though I have walked into something most mysterious since everyone stopped talking the moment I entered." One eyebrow arching, she smiled at him. "I do hope that someone will tell me what it is all about!"

Jonathan rose, as was polite, but his lips seemed no longer able to deliver speech. Even his breath seemed to have fixed itself inside his chest as he stared, his mouth ajar, at the beautiful young woman who had just walked in. Her skin was like alabaster, her lips a gentle pink, pulled into a soft smile as blue eyes sparkled back at him. He had nothing to say and everything to say at the very same time. Could this delightful young woman be Lady Yardley's cousin? And if she was, then why was no one introducing him?

"Allow me to introduce you." As though he had read his thoughts, Lord Yardley threw out one hand towards the young woman. "Might I present Lady Cassandra, daughter to the Earl of Holford. And this, Lady Cassandra, is my dear friend, the Marquess of Sherbourne. He is an excellent sort. You need have no fears with him."

Bowing quickly towards the young woman, Jonathan fought to find his breath.

"I certainly would not be so self-aggrandizing as to say

that I was 'an excellent sort', Lady Cassandra." he was somehow unable to draw his gaze away from her, and his heart leaped in his chest when she smiled all the more. "But I shall be the most excellent companion to you, should you require it, just as I am with Lord and Lady Yardley."

There was a breath of silence, and Jonathan cleared his throat, aware that he had just said more to her than he had ever said to any other young lady upon first making their acquaintance. Even Lord Yardley appeared to be a little surprised, for there was a blink, a smile and, after another long pause, the conversation continued. Lady Yardley gestured for her cousin to come and sit beside her, and the young lady obliged. Jonathan finally managed to drag his eyes away to another part of the room, only just becoming aware of how frantically his heart was beating. Everything he had just said to his friend regarding what would occur should he ever meet a young lady who stole his attention in an instant came back to him. Had he meant those words?

Giving himself a slight shake, Jonathan settled back into his chair, lost in thought as conversation flowed around the room. This was nothing more than an instant attraction, the swift kick of desire which would be gone within a few hours. There was nothing of any seriousness in such a swift response, he told himself. He had nothing to concern himself with and thus, he tried to insert himself back into the conversation just as quickly as he could.

Oh, no, Jonathan likes her! Perhaps he will have to change his mind about becoming leg-shackled! Check out the rest of story in the Kindle Store The Heart of a Gentleman

JOIN MY MAILING LIST

Sign up for my newsletter to stay up to date on new releases, contests, giveaways, freebies, and deals!

Free book with signup!

Monthly Facebook Giveaways! Books and Amazon gift cards!
Join me on Facebook: https://www.
facebook.com/rosepearsonauthor

Website: www.RosePearsonAuthor.com

Follow me on Goodreads: Author Page

Printed in Great Britain
by Amazon

26595406R00126